'Mr MacNamara,' Rae said heatedly, 'I don't particularly appreciate your silently branding me an emotionally shallow, romantically fickle, hard and heartless person because I happened to answer your ad.'

'It wasn't my ad,' he pointed out calmly.

'All right, then! I still don't think you have the least right to sit in judgement. You don't understand. You don't know my motivations . . . and you don't know me!'

'Why did you answer that ad?' he asked, his tone amiable enough, though the look of hard censure never left his eyes.

Oh-oh! She'd walked herself right into that one. She was hardly going to come off in a better light if she admitted she'd answered the ad to flesh out a magazine article!

MACNAMARA'S BRIDE

BY

QUINN WILDER

MILLS & BOON LIMITED
ETON HOUSE   18-24 PARADISE ROAD
RICHMOND   SURREY   TW9 1SR

*First published in Great Britain 1989
by Mills & Boon Limited*

© Quinn Wilder 1989

*Australian copyright 1989
Philippine copyright 1989
This edition 1989*

ISBN 0 263 76308 0

*Set in Baskerville 11 on 11 pt.
01-8905-48465*

Typeset in Great Britain by JCL Graphics, Bristol

Made and Printed in Great Britain

CHAPTER ONE

RAE DOUGLAS stared out of the plate-glass window of her posh twenty-third-floor office. The downtown landscape looked unbearably bleak to her. Calgary seemed colourless—a depressing assortment of greys. The sky was grey, the other office towers were grey, the street and the people scurrying along it far below her seemed dreary and washed out. The Bow River, which she could just glimpse through a tangle of concrete obstacles, looked icily cold and gloomy.

She shivered unconsciously. Would winter ever end? Officially it was already spring, but she had yet to spot a robin, or see blades of green grass pushing bravely through last year's dead covering. But in a moment of brutal self-honesty she wondered if spring *was* beginning its slow process of rebirth, and she had simply failed to notice, a prisoner of her inner self, caught in a web of perpetual winter . . .

Her own reflection, shadowily superimposed over the view, caught her attention and did nothing to alleviate her feelings of bleakness. Her thick, sandy-coloured hair had been cut severely short, a style that unfortunately emphasised the gauntness of her narrow face and made her sapphire-coloured eyes look too large and too sad, like those of an orphaned waif in a tacky painting.

'Well, Rae, I like the title. "Object: Matrimony" should grab a few readers.'

Rae's introspection ended abruptly, and she

swivelled around in her chair and regarded her boss wearily. It was a weak compliment, after all. Out of two thousand, five hundred words, Sal had liked two?

'What's wrong with it?' she forced herself to ask.

Sal sighed, tossed down the sheaf of papers, and crossed one silk-sheathed leg over the other. 'Nothing, exactly. Technically, it's a perfect article. You've covered several different angles, your facts are solid, your ''i''s dotted, ''t''s crossed.'

'And?' Rae prodded softly.

'And it's boring, Rae.' Sal slammed a manicured fist on to Rae's desk, her professional mask replaced with a look of annoyed exasperation. 'Dammit! It was supposed to be fun! It was supposed to be a rollicking and merry little story, and you were supposed to have a ball doing it. It had incredible potential: isolated Canadian farmers advertising in nationally respected agricultural magazines for wives? Why, the wildly romantic days of mail-order brides are not dead!

'But somehow you missed the essence: the adventure, the humour, the mystery, the romance. The only lively moment in your whole story is the verbatim ad you inserted from the guy who wanted to meet a woman with her own tractor—and requested a picture of the tractor! And the parts that should have been poignant weren't.' Sal held up a black and white photo accusingly. 'Look at these people.'

Rae looked. It showed an older couple she'd interviewed who had met through the personal column of an agricultural magazine, fallen in love, been happily married for years. They were leaning against each other, looking at each other with calf-like expressions of wonder and devotion etched into weatherbeaten faces.

They look like two people madly in love in this picture, don't they?' Sal pressed.

'I guess so,' Rae conceded, without enthusiasm.

'Then how come they don't sound like it in your story? They come across as flat and lifeless; dull as yesterday's porridge. They don't seem like the kind of adventurers who would answer a personal ad in a quest for a lifelong partner. There's something wrong. The people in your story don't match the people in this picture. What happened?'

'I didn't trust him!' Rae burst out, pointing at the man in the picture, and regretting it instantly when a look of sad knowing appeared on Sal's face.

'But why?' Sal asked softly. 'Did he make a pass at you, Rae? Did he ogle every woman who walked into the restaurant where the three of you had dinner that night? Did he mock his wife behind her back?'

'No, of course not,' Rae said hurriedly. 'I take it back. He was a nice man. They were a nice couple.' But even to her own ears she sounded unconvinced.

'So?'

'So, I just couldn't trust him, all right?' The anger that slipped by her vigilant guard into her words startled her. After all this time . . .

She tried again. 'I just couldn't believe that . . .' Her voice faded weakly, and she swivelled abruptly and looked out of her window.

'You couldn't believe that he wasn't seeing another woman. Isn't that right, Rae?' The words were gentle, and Rae turned slowly back, her blue eyes darkened with pain.

'You should have given this article to someone else, Sal. I told you that at the beginning.' Her tone was defeated.

'For God's sake, Rae! It's been nearly a year. How long are you going to insist on seeing Roger in every man? How long are you going to insist on punishing yourself?'

'Punishing myself?' Rae echoed, startled.

'Don't you see that's what you're doing? You're walking through life in a haze. You're making sure you don't give your heart any opportunity to mend. You don't go out. You don't make any effort to look attractive. Your apartment looks like hell. For God's sake, absolve yourself. It wasn't your fault! He was a despicable cad, and he took you for a roller-coaster ride. Kiss it goodbye, and get on with your life.'

Yes, some people would do that. Absolve themselves of all responsibility. Rae tried, not for the first time, to make Sal understand.

'But I should have known,' she said firmly. 'I should have realised.'

'It's over!'

'It's not,' Rae insisted quietly, 'because I'm still here. I was too easy to fool. I was a naïve idiot. I never guessed. I never even suspected. I really believed he loved me. I thought *we* were going to get married. Now I can't trust myself. How can I ever trust myself again?'

For a moment reality faded, and it wasn't Sal sitting across from her. It was a young woman trying to look composed, holding a squirming baby on her lap. 'I'm Pamela Whitney,' she'd said, and Rae had tried desperately to believe it was his sister or his sister-in-law. But the baby looked just like Roger. Winter had begun in that moment—with a young woman looking at her, her expression half accusing and half pleading. *Please leave my husband alone.*

'Rae?'

'Sorry,' she muttered.

'Rae, listen to me,' Sal said urgently, leaning forward. 'I don't think of myself as your boss, so much as your friend. But I'm beginning to wonder if protecting you isn't kind at all, but cruel.'

'Protecting me?'

'I'll lay it on the line, Rae. Your work isn't up to scratch and hasn't been for a long time. Yes, it's technically good, but technically good writers come a dime a dozen. You were hired by *Womanworld* because you had something else—you had a sparkle, a certain charm, a sort of tender touch to the way that you wrote that made everything you did so special. I can't believe that's gone, just because you haven't seen it for a long time. But I also can't continue to convince the other editors forever.'

A tender touch? Rae smiled derisively. If that had ever been a part of her, he had destroyed it. 'It's gone, Sal,' she said softly. Tender hearts only got hurt.

'Look, Rae, I wish there was a nicer way to put this——'

'But my job's on the line, right?'

Sal nodded miserably, then with obvious effort looked for a bright spot. 'Well, maybe there's still hope for "Object: Matrimony". Didn't you say you have one angle left to cover?'

Rae nodded, relieved they weren't going to dwell excessively on the subject of her shaky professional footing. She didn't want to contemplate joining the ranks of the jobless. The very idea left her inwardly shaking, though she forced herself to look businesslike.

'I answered a few of the ads.'

Sal's eyes widened appreciatively. 'You mean you answered them posing as a prospective bride?' At Rae's nod, she hooted. 'Now, that's *fun*! That could be just the angle to breathe some life into this piece.'

Rae didn't have the heart to tell her it hadn't been a sense of fun that had motivated her. She didn't know quite what it had been, though she suspected it was a suppressed need for revenge. She had been deceived—now she would deceive. She would be the one with the power to hurt—not the helpless victim.

Only life hadn't left her quite as hardened as she would have liked. Because, as she had looked through the eager replies to the responses she'd sent, she had one by one discarded them. The letters had revealed such an aching loneliness; in the accompanying pictures she had seen vulnerability, hopefulness, sincerity that she could not trust herself with. Except for one.

She rifled through her desk drawer, and handed Sal a colour snapshot and several typed notes. She took a deep, determined breath. 'I'm going to spend the weekend on this man's farm.'

Sal reached eagerly for the picture, and gasped. '*This* man is advertising for a wife? But, Rae, he's gorgeous.'

Rae nodded solemnly. Gorgeous. Invulnerable. A worthy opponent.

Sal handed the picture back. 'What's his name?'

'Galen MacNamara.'

Sal sighed girlishly. 'A fitting name for a Celtic chieftain.'

Rae's gaze was drawn irresistibly to the picture, though she had studied it long and hard more times than she cared to admit. There was an enigma here.

Men like this did not advertise for wives. They
fought off eager women with sticks—or ran a string
of them . . . as Roger had.

Not that the man resembled Roger in anything
more than that they were both undeniably
attractive, though in a far different way. Roger had
been, well, almost pretty, with his huge china-blue
eyes and his blond curling hair; the model of the
successful corporate golden boy in his three-piece
suits and diamond tie-pins.

The man in the snap was a different kind of
attractive—he looked as though he were a son of
black soil and sunshine, wind and rain. In the snap,
Galen MacNamara was leaning his elbows on the
top rail of a fence. There was an element of surprise
in his face, as though he'd been concentrating on
something on the other side of that fence and
somebody had called, 'Hey, Galen!' and clicked the
shutter just as he turned.

The lack of pose seemed to result in something of
the man's spirit being captured on film. Something
strongly mysterious and inviting that overrode the
faint bitter downturn of those firm, sensuous lips
and that compelled Rae to look at the picture again
and again.

His thick hair was red—not flaming, or orange,
but rather a burnished bronze. The wind was
sweeping it back from his high forehead. His
features were chiselled and rugged. A strong nose, a
firm chin, a stern line around his unsmiling mouth.
His eyes were very dark—she couldn't tell from the
picture whether they were a dark brown or black.
But again, there was something there she found
intriguing—a faint, challenging glitter glowing in
their depths. There were lines around his eyes, as if

once he had laughed often, and yet he no longer
looked like a man of laughter. His face was deeply
tanned, and not a sun-lamp or three-weeks-in-
Florida tan, but one caused by constant exposure to
the elements he looked so at home with—wind, rain,
sun or snow.

He wore a plaid shirt that pulled tightly over the
muscles of his upper arms, his shoulders and his
chest. Like the tan, the muscle struck her as being
the natural inheritance of a man whose work was
hard and physical—rather than the variety that was
built in gyms to impress at singles bars.

Bronze hair sprang thickly from where the shirt
opened at his neck. His figure tapered down to a flat
stomach, and narrow hips. Long, muscled legs were
outlined by the fabric of tight, faded jeans.

All in all, the picture he made was one of almost
intimidating strength. It was in the lines of his face,
and there again in the fluid line of his body.

'Not exactly modest, is he?'

Rae pulled herself unwillingly from the picture.
'What?'

Sal laughed and read the ad in her hand out loud.
' "Tall, handsome, hard-working farmer would like
to meet intelligent, attractive and interesting
woman. Object: matrimony. Please reply . . ." ' She
shuffled through the few typewritten notes he had
sent Rae, and the beginning of a frown started on
her face.

'I don't know, Rae,' she said, suddenly doubtful.
'These notes just don't look like something he'd
write. They're—what's the right way of putting
it—almost simple? Even the ad doesn't seem to suit
the man in the picture. Does it?'

'I didn't think so, either,' Rae admitted. 'But

then I started to think about it, and it occurred to me if he was perfect he sure as hell wouldn't be advertising for a wife. Maybe he's illiterate.' She smiled ruefully. 'Or maybe he's so shy in the presence of women that he stutters.'

'I don't know.' Sal shook her head thoughtfully. 'There's something untrustworthy about a man who types his signature. Tell me about this weekend.'

'Not much to tell. We exchanged a few short notes, and in his last one he suggested I come out to his farm for the weekend and I agreed.'

'Where is the farm?'

'Somewhere near Red Deer,' Rae tossed out carelessly.

'But that's not isolated,' Sal pointed out suspiciously.

Rae shrugged. 'Well, I'm committed now. He's coming to get me on Saturday afternoon.'

'Coming to get you? Why wouldn't you just drive yourself?'

'Sal, I'm the one who doesn't trust men, remember? I'm not driving myself because I'd probably get hopelessly lost on some country backroad. Besides, he really never offered a choice. He just wrote that he'd be at my place on Saturday at two.'

'I don't like it,' Sal said stubbornly.

'A few minutes ago you were telling me I had to learn to trust again,' Rae reminded her.

'But this sounds almost as if you don't care. As if you're placing yourself in a situation that could be potentially perilous, and you don't even care.'

'He is coming to the apartment. I promise, if he looks like a screwball I simply won't go.' She saw the look flash through Sal's eyes. It said, but you have

no judgement in men. Look at the last time. It said
that, even though Sal had tried to convince her only
moments ago that the whole Roger fiasco hadn't
been her fault. She felt as if Sal's real feelings were
showing now.

Rae smiled tightly. 'Well, if I end up dead, you
have his name, don't you?' And then she wondered
if it had really gone that far. If she simply didn't care
any more—about anything.

By Saturday afternoon Rae was feeling haggard and
out of sorts. She had barely slept Friday night,
worrying if Sal might be right, wondering if she had
unwittingly set herself up as a victim for a demented
psycho. In the middle of the night she'd got up and
checked the postmarks on his letters to make sure he
really was from around Red Deer. Then she had
called directory enquiries and got his phone number.
He existed. As far as she could tell, he was who he
claimed to be. A psycho killer would not leave a trail
that was so easy to follow. Besides, she needed this
story. She needed it desperately.

She couldn't afford to lose her job, not financially,
and, more importantly, not emotionally. Her career
was the only thing that even rippled the surface of
her lethargy and forced her out of bed in the
mornings.

Weary now, she took out his picture and looked at
it again. She wasn't sure what a pervert looked like,
but surely not like this? On the other hand, Roger
hadn't looked like the kind who would have a wife
and child secreted away, either.

Still, she finally decided to wait until he arrived at
her apartment. If she felt even a twinge of
uncertainty, then she could suggest an alternative

plan. He could stay in Calgary and wine and dine her in the safety of public places.

It wouldn't make as good a story, she thought dejectedly, but at least she realised that she hadn't given up on life all together. It was the strange haze that she moved in that had prevented her from taking proper precautions—not a secret death wish. Reassured that she wouldn't have to make an appointment with a psychiatrist just yet, she finally drifted off to sleep.

Now, waiting on Saturday afternoon for her apartment intercom to announce the arrival of her visitor, she had to admit she was still nervous, for all she tried to convince herself she had nothing to fear. She checked her appearance for the fourth time. Was it right for a farm? It was imperative that she look the role of a woman really interested in living on a farm. She wasn't sure her designer jeans quite gave that impression, but on the other hand, she doubted many men knew the difference between Levis and Calvin Klein, anyway. Had she known what was at stake, she might have put a little more time into preparing a convincing wardrobe.

She wore the jeans with an oversized cream-coloured Angora sweater, and decided the outfit would do. If it wasn't exactly rural, it wasn't exactly big-city either. Casual, muted, faintly flattering.

She realised, with a start, that it was the first time in a long while that she had spent any kind of energy or effort debating over what to wear, the first time in a long while that she had turned in front of her mirror regarding her slim figure critically this way and that, trying to imagine what kind of reaction she would elicit from masculine eyes.

It was the first time she'd wished back the long,

heavy hair that Roger had loved so much, that had
softened the effect of the cheekbones a touch too
high, a chin a touch too pointed. Still, the new cut
did reveal the long, sensuous line of her neck, and
the delicate shape of her face. And in other times she
might not have minded that her eyes looked so
prominent. It was only that now they looked dull
and without sparkle. Did her eyes always look that
sad? she wondered, turning abruptly away from the
hurt look, far too similar to that of a trusting dog
who'd been kicked. She was annoyed that it
mattered to her. The story was the priority, and
Galen's response to her should matter only in that
context.

He was very late. Where was he? At half-past
three she decided she wasn't going anywhere with
him—if he ever showed up. She hated people who
couldn't be punctual. The whole idea had been
crazy anyway. She'd just have to prove herself with
a different article, though the very thought made her
realise she was already attached to this one, counting
on it, sensing in it the element that was needed to
make her writing come back to life.

She sighed. Her mood had not been much
improved by the fact that she had hauled out back
issues of *Womanworld* to help her pass the time. She
hoped to find a few redeeming qualities in her
articles of the last few months. Instead, Rae found
Sal had been absolutely right. Her articles were as
dull as dead carp.

Finally, there was a knock on her door. Rae
started and then scowled. How had her mystery man
managed to bypass the electronic security buzzers?
If it was her mystery man.

She got up quietly and peered out of her peephole.

Her irritation grew. No one was in the hallway. She had never particularly appreciated the humour of ducking out of sight of the peephole, and she decided right then and there that she had had enough of Galen MacNamara—without ever laying eyes on the real thing. Not only was he late, he was given to playing silly games. Well, maybe she would play her own game and just pretend she wasn't home. That would teach him to be late. He could just go away, and she could just forget she had ever had this insane idea.

But, even as she started to turn from the door, she had to admit she was just the slightest bit sorry she wouldn't be meeting that enigmatic man in the picture, after all—in fact, it was taking an amazing amount of will-power to turn from that door when she knew it must be him on the other side. It's because of the article, she told herself fiercely.

Abruptly, she decided to give him one more chance to show himself and turned her eye back to the tiny porthole in her door. But it wasn't the strong features of Galen MacNamara that she encountered. It was five small and rather grubby fingers stretched frantically up towards her peephole.

Rae opened the door, and looked down. An elfin face looked back up at her. She guessed the boy to be six or maybe seven. He was an authentic carrot-top, and his face was covered with blotches of freckles.

'I waved at you so you would know it wasn't a mugger-man,' he informed her. 'I'm not tall enough for you to see me through the look-out hole.' He regarded her solemnly. 'Gramps says you have to be careful of stuff like that in the city—mugger-mens—did you think I was one?' He made an obvious effort not to sound too hopeful.

Something about his eyes struck her as oddly
familiar. They danced mischievously, so dark that
she couldn't tell if they were brown or black.

'Well, I thought you could have been a mugger,'
she conceded, straight-faced.

'Gramps got lost,' he informed her chattily, 'and
cussed real good. My dad washes my mouth out
with soap if I cuss. This is a real big city. Gramps is
looking for a parking spot. I think if my dad was
here, he'd wash *his* mouth out with soap. We almost
had an accident.'

'Really?' she asked a little weakly. What did this
charming little character want? Bottles? Newsprint?
He was silent now, scrutinising her solemnly. He
sighed.

'You aren't as pretty as you were in the picture.'

'Billy, that ain't the type of thing you tell a lady.'

Rae lifted her eyes from the rather captivating
leprechaun face, and saw an old man. His sparse
hair was white as ivory, his face was leathery and
creased, he was dressed in a rumpled jean jacket and
jeans. Two blue eyes twinkled merrily at her, and he
smiled a shy, gap-toothed smile, and extended his
hand.

'Sorry, we're late, ma'am. Kyle MacNamara.'

The light went on in her head, and her eyes raced
back to Billy. Of course. She should have recognised
it immediately. The stubborn set of the chin, the
shape of the cheekbones, and the eyes. Especially the
eyes.

She almost laughed out loud. She'd been worried
about being abducted by a pervert? But why hadn't
Galan MacNamara told her their weekend would be
chaperoned? For that matter, why hadn't he

informed her about his extended family? That seemed like a rather large detail for a wife-hunting man to leave out. Could these two charmers have something to do with Galen MacNamara having to advertise for a wife? She was beginning to feel delighted, and a heading formed in her mind: 'Bachelor farmer springs ready-made family on mail-order bride.' The story wasn't going to be just good—it was going to be great!

'Galen got tied up with something and couldn't come himself,' the old man told her. 'Calfing season,' he added, as though that explained everything. 'Have you got a bag, or something?'

'Yes. I'll just get it.'

The old man stepped inside, crusty dignity in every line of his face. 'I'll get it.'

She hid a smile at the old-world chivalry and pointed to her bedroom. Billy slipped in the door and looked around with interest. His face fell. 'Boy, this place is a dump.'

She followed his gaze and acknowledged that he only spoke the truth. After Roger, she had swept away from her life everything he had ever touched, and replaced it carelessly, if at all. For the first time she felt a tweak of embarrassment at the way she had allowed herself to slip. Maybe Sal had had a point. Was she punishing herself? Didn't she feel she any longer had the right to nice furniture and beautiful surroundings? She touched her hair self-consciously. The right to be attractive?

'I'm planning on getting some new things soon,' she surprised herself by murmuring.

'You won't have to if you marry my dad,' she was told with deadly earnest.

She stared down at his hopeful face, shocked.

Somehow, with the arrival of the MacNamara clan on her doorstep, and her eagerness for the story, the reality of this weekend had been swept from her mind. Now, her deceit turned sour in her mouth. It had seemed all right when she had thought that the self-assured man in the picture was the only one involved . . .

She shrugged away the thoughts. Certainly Galen MacNamara hadn't planned on proposing after one weekend, anyway. She would collect the facts she needed and slip from his life before the boy or anybody else pinned too many hopes on her.

The old man led the way down to a battered old pick-up truck, and they all squeezed in. Within seconds the boy was asleep, his head burrowed comfortably into her shoulder.

'He's been pretty excited about all this,' Gramps explained, looking gently at the boy as he drove with erratic nonchalance through the bustling city. 'He didn't mean it, either, about your not being pretty. Your hair's different. That's probably all he meant.'

Rae smiled. 'The picture I sent was taken a long time ago, Mr MacNamara. I feel as if I've changed.' Inside. Outside.

'Call me Gramps.' He was silent for a minute. 'When I saw that picture, I couldn't figure out why such a pretty young thing would write away for a husband. But now, seeing you in person, I understand better. You've got a ''run-over-by-a-tractor'' look, and I guess that's as good a reason as any.'

A run-over-by-a-tractor look? Rae made a half-hearted attempt to feel offended, but found she couldn't manage it. In fact, an amused smile was tugging on her lips.

'Nope, it's not a bad thing at all, needin' someone or something to help heal the wounds,' he mused, then hesitated before continuing softly, 'Galen's got wounds, too. Maybe you could remember that.'

Her amusement died. 'Oh.' That impervious man in the picture, wounded? In the back of her mind she wondered if she had still plotted to revenge herself at his expense, if this amazingly astute little man beside her had somehow seen through her. It was easy to imagine there had been a soft note of plea in his words.

A restless night, the motion of the truck, the wailing of some sad cowboy over the radio, a little boy's head tucked trustingly into her arm—she was asleep before she could contemplate the question further.

CHAPTER TWO

RAE and Billy both woke up when Gramps stopped to put fuel in the truck on the outskirts of Red Deer. When he turned on to a gravel road she began to feel relieved that she had not attempted to undertake the journey on her own. He would come to a crossroads and turn, a crossroads and turn, until Rae felt hopelessly lost in a draughtboard maze of criss-crossing country roads. Her interest in the landscape soon died. It seemed every bit as bleak and colourless as the landscape of downtown Calgary.

The large, flat squares of farmland were interspersed with groves of trees, dead-looking and leafless. Even the stands of evergreens looked grey-washed from dust and snow. The fields were muddy, spotted with banks of dirty-looking melting snow.

The only brightness was provided by Billy's constant stream of chatter. He talked about school and his friends, his teacher, his pets, his projects. He hopped from subject to subject with the irrepressible energy of a bouncing bunny.

'Almost there,' Gramps announced, sliding a look at her face. 'Actually, you couldn't see this countryside at a worse time of year. It's beautiful in every other season. It will be again in a few weeks.'

So why hadn't Galen waited to show her his home in a better light? she wondered acidly. So far the mystery man was scoring no points at all for effort.

'Here we are,' Gramps proclaimed, turning on to

yet another gravel road. This one twisted through a
grove of trees and crossed a small, picturesque log
bridge. Rae looked down as they crossed over. The
waters of a swollen creek seemed to be just about
touching the bottom planks of the bridge.

'Isn't the water awfully high?' she ventured.

'Sure is,' Gramps agreed, and Billy tittered. They
both seemed highly satisfied with the water level,
and Rae shrugged it off as having something to do
with the farm.

Billy was looking at the sky, frowning. 'But,
Gramps, it doesn't look like it's going to——'

'Shush, boy,' Gramps said warningly.

Rae, too, looked at the sky. Alberta's boast of
almost constantly blue skies did not hold true
today—had not held true all spring. But the layer of
grey overhead did not seem to hold moisture, either.
'Do you need rain?'

A rather conspiratorial look passed between the
young boy and the old man.

'Depends on who you ask, I guess,' Gramps
drawled.

They were driving through another grove of trees,
and suddenly they burst into the open.

Rae gasped with unexpected pleasure. There,
against all the greys, was a haven of gold. The house
was constructed of logs. Even on this cold and
dreary day the polished surface of the wood seemed
to radiate a warmth of its own. The house itself was
two-storey, beautifully designed with a surrounding
porch on the ground floor and gabled windows on
the second.

'It's beautiful,' she breathed with delight.

'We done it ourselves,' Billy confided proudly.
'Me and my dad and Gramps.'

She filed that interesting piece of information and
her eyes drifted beyond the house, which sat at the
edge of the tree grove. Far behind it was the classic
red barn and several outbuildings. Beyond that were
sweeping fields dotted with fat red and white cattle.

Gramps had taken her bag and moved towards
the house. She found a small hand nestled in hers.

'We're going to use the front door because you're
company,' Billy told her as he pulled her along the
flagstone path that led to the house.

She stopped again inside the front door, letting the
golden light seep into her very bones. The open-
beamed living-room was large, furnished with
comfortable-looking pieces that had a distinctive air
that made her suspect they had been hand-hewn by
a master craftsman. High, cathedral-style windows
faced out into the trees. An open staircase off to one
side led to the second storey of the house.

'Like it?' Billy asked eagerly.

She could only nod mutely. 'Like' would have
been the understatement of the century. She loved
the room. She'd felt a rush of warmth and peace that
moment she had walked in the door. She'd felt an
inappropriate sense of homecoming that she had
never felt upon entering her mother's thoroughly
modern apartment where she had grown up.

For a moment she found herself almost wishing
she *had* entered this house as an innocent young
woman looking for a potential husband. She would
have been so thrilled with the house this man, who
was a stranger to her, had built. The hand-built
furniture and his magnificent home revealed a great
deal about him. She felt a vague danger from her
thoughts, and forced herself to look at the situation
professionally. Her delighted surprise might trans-

late into a good way to lead off her story . . .

'Billy, take Miss Douglas to the kitchen and make some coffee. I'll store her bags.'

'Rae, to both of you, please.'

The kitchen was as cosy and cheerful as the living-room. Rae watched in amazement as Billy got a chair and began expertly spooning coffee into the coffemaker.

'I cook, too,' he told her proudly when she expressed her surprise.

'What can you cook?' she asked patronisingly. 'Hot dogs?'

'That's baby stuff,' he informed her scornfully, and began to reel off a long list of his culinary conquests.

Gramps joined them and they sipped excellent coffee. But where was Galen? she wondered. He certainly wasn't giving the impression of being too excited about the arrival of his prospective bride. In fact, save for his extraordinary house, he was still scoring nil for effort. Didn't he have the sensitivity to realise how nerve-racking this experience would be to a stranger who would be meeting for the first time the man who might become her husband? Again, she tried to tell herself she wasn't taking it personally, only making notes for her article.

She glanced at Billy and Gramps, a little startled with how much affection she already felt for the pair of them. Surely they couldn't have anything to do with Galen MacNamara's difficulty in finding wife material on his own? The mystery around the man was mounting unbearably.

She was just about to ask the whereabouts of her host, when the door behind her opened, letting in a blast of chilly air. She twisted in her chair.

He looked just as he had in the picture, and yet Rae felt oddly unprepared for his real-life presence.

His bronze hair still looked wind-ruffled, his face exquisitely sculpted in stone. He was a big man, untouched by the perils of middle-age spread, his body looking as hard and firm as though it had been cast from molten steel. He was an exquisite specimen of the male animal, and her heart did an unexpected flip-flop within her chest—something she had sworn it would never do again.

Though his features remained impassive, something flickered in those dark eyes when his gaze met hers and held. She had the unfortunate sensation he was not in the least pleased with what he saw. What had he been expecting? she wondered desperately. The picture she had sent hadn't been *that* inaccurate.

'Hi, Dad.'

She glanced at Billy and frowned. There was something just a little too forced in the casualness of his greeting, in the bright charm of his smile.

'Hi, son.' Galen MacNamara's coal-black gaze had not left her face. Well, he didn't stutter, she told herself, a weak inner attempt at humour in a situation that was making her increasingly uncomfortable. Maybe her discomfort had something to do with the fact his voice was deeply sensual: velvet. There had to be a flaw somewhere. Where was it?

She reminded herself sharply that she was a professional writer, and that it had been a long time since meeting anyone had intimidated her. Still, when she stood up, she found herself trying to inconspicuously wipe her hand on her jeans before extending it.

'I'm Rae Douglas,' she introduced herself.

She expected him to say, 'Yes, I know.' Instead he met her grip, her hand disappearing inside one that was warm and incredibly strong. She felt an unwanted tingle of pure physical reaction. But his gaze remained aloof, and quizzical, as though her presence here was baffling and inexplicable—an unwanted intrusion into his male domain.

'What exactly brings you here, Ms Douglas?' he asked smoothly, releasing her hand and turning for coffee. Her mouth fell open and she stared at his broad back incredulously.

Well, there was the flaw. The man was obviously a victim of some form of mental disorder. He didn't know who she was, and he didn't remember inviting her. He obviously didn't even remember placing the ad. She turned and looked helplessly at Gramps, only to find him studying his feet with a great deal of interest. Why hadn't he warned her his son was not quite all there? His oblique reference to a 'wounding' returned, but she felt that was hardly fair and sufficient warning. Her gaze moved hopefully to Billy, but he too was oddly silent, looking out of the window with an oblivious gaze. Had the poor kid developed a defence system that allowed him to ignore the fact that his father was ill?

Unsupported, she turned back to find Galen looking at her expectantly, his penetrating black gaze making her feel like a fly pinned to a piece of paper. Her discomfort seemed to faintly amuse him. The sparkling eyes struck her as holding the promise of keen intellect and shrewdness. His did not seem to be the gaze of a bewildered, befuddled man.

'Mr MacNamara,' she said as gently as possible, giving him the benefit of the doubt, though vague derisiveness in his gaze made her want to snap shrewishly, 'don't you remember placing——'

'She's a friend of mine!' Gramps burst out behind her.

'She's the new music teacher!' Billy cried simultaneously.

Rae whirled and glared incredulously at both of them. Was this house full of madmen? Or were Billy and Gramps trying to protect Galen from the knowledge of his own serious impairment? She turned back to study Galen, no longer sure who was crazy. There was the unsettling possibility that all these people were normal, and something in her had finally snapped after the emotional pressure of the last long months.

Galen, thankfully, had removed his relentless gaze from her face and was now studying his father and his son with narrowed eyes. Moving with the deceptive slowness of a cat about to pounce, he pulled out a chair at the table and sat down. He took a sip of his coffee, his gaze continuing to move steadily from Gramps to Billy.

Rae stood for a moment longer, then awkwardly slid back into her seat. Gramps and Billy refused to look at her, or at Galen. They were now both totally engrossed in an inspection of the tips of their shoes. Their expressions were distinctly guilty, and Rae felt her confusion dissolving. Why, the pair of troublemakers had——

'Out with it.'

Galen's voice was soft as silk, but everyone else at the table, including Rae, jumped nervously.

'Out with what?' Gramps asked, his voice and expression a theatrical mixture of innocence and indignation.

'I want to know what mischief you two are into now.'

Galen's voice remained quiet, sure, and extremely authoritative.

The two conspirators exchanged one more guilty glance, and then Billy looked down at his hands.

'Boy, are you going to be mad,' he offered in a small voice.

'It's a good one, is it?'

Rae was astonished to see a faint upward quirk in that firm mouth, the smallest hint of amusement dance across dark eyes. For an absurd moment she believed Galen MacNamara was the most attractive man she had ever laid eyes on. But then his expression was quashed. It happened so quickly, she wasn't entirely sure she had seen it at all.

'Now, Galen, the boy just wanted a mother.' Gramps' tone was so low it was rendered nearly inaudible.

The silence was electric. 'The boy wanted a *what*?'

Reluctantly, Gramps fished a rather tattered scrap of glossy magazine paper from his shirt pocket and passed it to Galen.

Rae had an irresistible urge to laugh at his expression as she watched him scan the brief ad. He seemed to be paralysed by utter disbelief, and then red began to creep up the powerful column of his neck.

Oh dear, she thought, his whole masculine dignity has been offended. A renegade chortle escaped her.

He glared at her, and she apologetically covered her mouth with her hand, though there was nothing she could do about the shaking of her shoulders. She couldn't believe this was happening to her. Her sense of humour had died when her romance with Roger had died—she had frustrated an army of people who tried to cheer her up with teasing and

practical jokes by being unable to do more tha
smile wanly at their efforts.

And yet now laughter, as warm as a breath
spring, was glowing deep in her belly and she simp
could not stop it. But what Galen's furious, quellir
glare—the fact that this intimidating mountain of
man was a victim of such high jinks only made
funnier—couldn't accomplish, Billy's tears coul
The rumbles died within her.

'I just wanted a mommy,' he wailed, echoir
Gramps' words. Raè was reminded of how young
really was, despite the fact that he could make coff
and cook. He was, after all, just a little more than
baby. How could he possibly face the fury of t
man seated beside her? She turned to Galen, feelir
oddly like a mother lioness prepared to go to batt
for her cub. But with relief she realised that wouldn
be necessary.

The red had crept back down Galen's neck, ar
his harsh features had softened. His eyes were
longer cold—but turned velvet by the sadness of
man doing his best, and still failing. It was terrible
see a man of this power, a man so obvious
accustomed to ordering his universe, helple
against a small boy's need for tenderness of the kir
only a woman would be able to give.

Once again, she glimpsed something that gave
to the overpowering impression of invulnerability,
confidence, that she had first seen in that pictur
seen again when he first strolled into the room wi
such easy and sinewy grace. Rather than detractir
from the first impression, she found this hint of h
humanity somewhat devastating. It made him f
more attractive that his heart was not moulded fro
the same granite as his face.

'Come here, son.'

Rae expected he might hesitate, but Billy scurried around the table, and clambered up into his father's lap. Strong arms, corded with muscle, closed around him. She felt another breath of warmth, at the picture they made. The big man's strength tempered to gentleness as he, without a hint of self-consciousness, cuddled his son. Billy obviously felt not a speck of fear for this rather fearsome man, and Rae felt something tingle within her. It was refreshing to see a man so supremely confident in his masculinity that he tried to prove nothing, a man so sure of his strength that he did not feel driven to loud words and a show of complete lack of feelings to prove to the world and himself that he was not weak.

'Now, tell me why you wanted a mother,' Galen encouraged softly, his tone reinforcing all the conclusions Rae had just drawn, though she felt suddenly like an intruder on a very private family scene. But since she didn't know how to escape gracefully, and nobody seemed to remember she was there, she remained rooted to her chair.

Billy wiped a tear from his face, leaving a streak of grime. ''Cause we're making a Mother's Day present at school, and I don't have anyone to give mine to, and 'cause all the moms come in and help in our class and I don't have one to come, and 'cause Jake Andrews' mom smells so nice, and looks so pretty and makes the best chocolate chip cookies . . .' His voice faded away into a little hiccup.

'Those are all pretty good reasons for wanting a mom,' Galen commented gravely, and Rae felt a totally unwanted stab of tenderness for the big man. 'But what you did was wrong, son. We talk our problems over in this family, don't we? We don't just go ahead and try to solve things ourselves, especially when other people are involved. You should have come to me, and we would have talked about it, and maybe decided something together.'

'But then you might have married somebody I didn't like,' Billy responded stoutly.

Just from the emphasis he placed on 'somebody', Rae realised that there must be a woman in Galen's life already—and that Billy did not like her at all. In fact, maybe it was because he intuitively recognised that his dad was getting serious about that 'somebody' that he had taken matters into his own hands. The fact that he had been able to enlist his grandfather's aid must mean that Kyle MacNamara wasn't crazy about 'somebody' either.

'So did that give you the right to choose for me? Someone *I* don't like?'

Rae gasped indignantly. Galen didn't even know *her*. How dared he insinuate, on the weight of a few seconds' conversation, that he didn't like her? Mentally, she retracted each of the nice things she had just thought about him.

'Rae's real nice, Dad,' Billy said hopefully.

'I'm sure she is,' his father responded, not attempting to inject even a trace of conviction into his soft, powerful voice. 'But she'll be going home tonight. People should love each other very much before they decide to get married, son. You don't shop for a mate in the newspaper as if you were going to a shoe sale.'

His eyes rested on her for a moment, full of recrimination. She tilted her nose haughtily upward. No point in letting him think that his self-righteous opinion mattered one iota to her.

'I think we should at least ask Miss Douglas to

stay for supper, since we've put her to all this trouble,' Gramps suggested innocently. Rae couldn't help but wonder what the crafty old curmudgeon was up to now. She suspected he wasn't surrendering his role as matchmaker that easily.

Galen slid his son off his knee. 'Go and wash your face.' When the boy departed, Galen faced his father, the fury once again licking at the ebony surface of his eyes. 'I can understand a kid getting involved in such foolishness, but Dad, you should have known better. An ad in a magazine—good God in heaven, man!'

'So happens I think the boy needs a mother, too,' Gramps returned stubbornly.

'And you were going to pick her out?' The quiet, even voice held the sting of a whip.

'Well, the one you got your eye on now ain't good with the boy. 'Sides which, she'd have me rushed off to an old folks' home so fast it'd make my head spin.'

'You're talking complete nonsense,' Galen said with tight control. 'I don't know what Clarice does to get you two cooking up these wild notions about her.'

'And I don't know what she does to blind you to the fact she's a sharp-toothed shark looking for a sucker,' the old man came back bluntly and unapologetically.

For a long moment the two men glared at each other, and then Galen seemed to suddenly recall that a stranger shared their table and he flashed his father a final angry look. 'We'll talk about this later,' he promised crisply. 'Meanwhile, I'm sure Ms Douglas has no wish to have supper here, since she's

discovered this is one hardworking farmer who is not
the least bit interested in her as wife material. I'll
take her back to——' He looked at her
questioningly.

'Calgary,' she supplied, and then blinked sweetly
at him, 'and I'd simply love to have supper here.'

His expression blackened, and she nearly laughed
out loud again, since he was so obviously tempted to
order her out of his house and on her way. She could
feel the effort of his restraint when he managed to
nod.

'If that's what you'd like,' he said coolly, his black
eyes contemptuous, 'though I don't see what it
would accomplish.' His gaze branded her a silly and
desperate woman if she harboured any hopes that
her staying would soften him to his family's
ambitions for her.

'Accomplish?' she said sweetly. 'I happen to be
starving.'

His eyes narrowed and swept her face, and then
he picked up his coffee-cup, dismissing her, letting
her know he was not in any danger from her charms
because he found her charmless. She was more
insulted than she could ever remember being, and
hid the fact by raising an eyebrow carelessly at him,
as if his rudeness had been noted, and left her quite
unmoved.

For a brief moment their eyes held, clashed. She
felt the full force of his power, and was shaken by it.
She refused to look away, and could only hope that
she was managing a look of uncaring amusement in
the face of his irritation at her being here, his
contempt for the reason she had come to be here, his
aggravation that she was not bowing out gracefully.

He broke the hold he had on her eyes abruptly,

drained his coffee from the cup and stood up with an unconscious stretch that rippled pleasingly along the hard line of his body.

'I have work to do,' he said tonelessly, without adding a goodbye, or a 'see you later'. He turned and walked out the door, the only sign of his displeasure evident in the stiffness of the very broad back that was presented to her. His disapproving presence, she noted uneasily, lingered long after he had disappeared. She wished she had not agreed to stay to supper. The tension the man created in her was exhausting. Only now, after he'd been gone a full five minutes, did she feel herself beginning to relax.

Gramps silently refilled both their coffee-mugs, then sat down and looked at her contritely, though she could have sworn a certain mirth lurked in his eyes. She would have bet the old devil still had a card up his sleeve, although for the life of her she couldn't have guessed what it might be. Galen MacNamara was not allowing anybody to choose a wife for him—of that she was certain!

'I'm sorry, Rae. Can you forgive Billy and me?'

Somehow she managed to look stern. 'Gramps, a prank like this might be forgivable in a young boy, but a man of your age should have known better. It's quite inexcusable.'

'It weren't never a prank,' he told her softly. 'That boy needs a mother.'

'Yes, but his mother is going to have to be Galen's wife,' she reminded him patiently.

'Well, Galen needs a wife as much as the boy needs a mother,' the old man declared adamantly. 'Man's turning as sour as month-old milk.'

She couldn't have agreed with him more on his

last point, but she fought down the smile that threatened her lips. 'Er, Clarice hasn't prevented him from turning sour?'

'Are you kidding?' Gramps wrinkled his nose expressively. 'Now there's a woman who could curdle cream with a glance. And crafty! She's kind of crept into Galen's life until he just takes her being around for granted, and when he least expects it, she's gonna thump him over the head and drag him off to the altar! Nope, Billy and me decided Galen needs a little something to shake him up and out of a dangerously comfortable habit.'

'And that little something is me?' She would have given her right arm to hear Galen's explanation of his relationship with Clarice. She somehow doubted that he would describe it as a comfortable habit. He did not have the appearance of a man given to 'comfortable habits'. No, those dark, dark eyes smouldered with a promise of virility and passion—not a newspaper, a pair of slippers, an old dog and a pipe in front of a fire. He *was* the fire!

'Well——' Gramps hedged uncomfortably.

'Oh, Gramps, what on earth did you expect to happen once you had me here? Did you think that he was just going to fall instantly and madly in love with me, get down on one knee and propose we spend the rest of our lives together? I mean, didn't either you or Billy think beyond the point of getting me here? I'm not stunning enough to clear a man's mind of every woman but me! And you must have known how Galen would react to this kind of meddling in his life. And he would have reacted that way even if he had felt an instant attraction to me—which he certainly did not.'

The admission made her feel oddly pained, but

only, she told herself firmly, because she had had a
hidden agenda for this weekend, article aside. It was
going to be fairly hard to revenge herself on the male
gender with a man who was not in the least
interested in her. Yes, that was her only reason to be
stung by Galen's animosity towards her.

'Galen's like a dog with an old bone to gnaw on,'
Gramps said, frowning at her disbelieving giggle.
'He thinks he's happy enough. Then you throw him
a new bone. Well, he's stubborn. He ain't even
gonna look at it. But next thing you know he's
sneaking the odd little sniff——'

'Enough!' Rae pleaded, having nearly collapsed
with laughter at the unimaginable analogy.

'All I'm trying to say is that he can be a bit of a
hothead. But if he cools down and gets a chance to
know you better, he'll like you. Billy and I picked
you from over a hundred women who responded.'

'I'm flattered,' she said with surprised sincerity,
'but it's all for naught, Gramps. He's not going to
cool down before supper, and I suspect I'll be
hustled out of here as fast as he can manage. I'll
probably still have my dessert spoon in hand.'

And, hidden agenda aside, there went the article,
she realised with a sigh. She tried not to feel panic.
What would she do without her job? She felt the
black pit her life had become swelling up,
threatening to swallow her whole.

Gramps misinterpreted her sigh, and patted her
hand reassuringly. 'I don't believe you'll be going
quite as quick as all that,' he told her mysteriously.

She shook her head helplessly. 'In that case, I
don't think you know your son nearly as well as you
think.'

'Oh, I know my son. More important, I know the

weather.' His gaze went to the window, and he
sniffed the air like an old wolf. 'Storm coming,' he
announced with satisfaction. 'One hell of a storm.'

Her own grandmother had once predicted
weather changes by the feeling in her bones. As far
as Rae could remember, her accuracy had been
about zero. Besides, she didn't see what a storm had
to do with Galen and herself. At most it would delay
her exit by a few hours. And the only reason she'd
care to stay anyway was to get material for her
article, and yes, to bring the arrogant man-
mountain down a peg or two—motives that certainly
weren't in keeping with Gramps' romantic plans.

Billy bounced back into the room, the grime
streak intact on his face. 'See my transformer?' he
crowed at Rae. 'Look, I'll show you what it does.'

While he showed her and talked non-stop.
Gramps began to prepare dinner. He refused to be
rushed—in fact, Rae could have sworn he was
dawdling purposely—despite the fact that his
intimidating son had returned from outside and his
impatience could be felt even though he was in the
next room doing something. Every now and then he
would look in, a scowl furrowing his features, and
growl either about starving to death or wanting to
return from Calgary some time before dawn if
nobody minded.

Gramps ignored him, but Rae found herself
uncomfortably aware of him, aware of the angry
rustle of papers from the room next door. Each time
he poked his head in the kitchen door she was
startled anew by the force of him—animal,
magnetic, mysterious. She wished again that she
had not accepted the invitation. Her confidence was
so weak now anyway, and it did not help to be so

thoroughly ignored by a man she found impossible to ignore.

Billy became increasingly quiet as night fell, looking anxiously to the window over and over again, and then almost accusingly to his grandfather. So he, too, had been informed a storm was in the wind, Rae surmised, and shook her head at the rather shaky plans of the matchmakers. It seemed their whole plot relied just a touch too heavily on the weather conditions. And she wished Gramps hadn't got the boy's hopes up over such a frail possibility.

She realised suddenly that it was a good thing she was leaving tonight. It would be far too easy to get involved in this family, too easy to care about Billy and Gramps.

It was eight by the time Gramps placed a succulent roast chicken on the table. The meal was delicious, though Rae's enjoyment was somewhat curbed by the oppressive silence at the table. She made one or two efforts at conversation and then gave up. Billy wouldn't be drawn out, Gramps seemed preoccupied, and Galen was grouchily monosyllabic. Finally, she didn't even dare look up from her plate, because when she did her eyes always drifted to him, and wanted to stay fastened on him, as if a long, leisurely study of his tantalisingly remote features would help her unlock the enigma, the mystery of his attractiveness.

Suddenly Billy cocked an ear, and a grin split his face from ear to ear. Rae stopped eating and listened, for a moment hearing nothing, and then hearing the lonely, awesome howl of the wind. Billy jumped up and ran to the window just as the first drops of moisture were being blown violently against it.

'It's storming,' he announced triumphantly.

'Oh, hell!' Galen tossed down his napkin and joined his son at the window. In a minute Rae sat at the large table by herself, because Gramps, too, was at the window.

'That rain's gonna turn to snow,' Gramps declared authoritatively. 'Wouldn't be at all surprised if what he have here is gonna be one heck of a spring blizzard.'

'Nonsense,' Galen said tightly. 'It'll be over in ten minutes.'

But in ten minutes the storm outside had worsened, and now the occasional snowflake was mixed in with the rain.

'If I didn't know better,' Galen muttered, glaring at his grinning son, and his smug father, 'I'd say you two planned this somehow. Fortunately, I'm a reasonable man and I know there's a limit to what even the two of you can do.' His gaze flicked to Rae, cold and angry. She did not feel it was the gaze of a reasonable man.

By the end of dinner his face was like thunder. The storm had thickened outside the window and Gramps was telling prairie blizzard stories about men who had got lost between their houses and their barns in the swirling, disorientating snowstorms.

'Yup, when I was a boy, I can remember having a rope tied to my waist to go out to the barn to feed the stock. Ain't seen a blizzard like that for years, mind, but this one sure is brewing up——'

'If this is intended to sway me into staying here tonight,' Galen interjected with dry resignation, laced faintly with impatience, 'you can start winding down. We won't be going anywhere until morning.'

'I'll show you the farm in the morning,' Billy

offered happily. 'There's new kittens, and my horse, and the tree-house——'

'There won't be time,' his father cut him off coldly. 'We'll be leaving first thing in the morning.'

'No, you won't,' Billy said confidently. ''Cause——'

'Shush, boy,' Gramps said sternly. Galen looked at them both suspiciously, then shook his head wearily, and let it pass.

CHAPTER THREE

'WELL, young man, time for your bath and bed,' Gramps told Billy.

They had retired to the living-room after dinner, and it was yet another room that impressed Rae with its warmth and charm. One wall was completely book-lined, another almost completely comprised of large sliding glass doors. This room was obviously the family centre. It held a desk, the size and heaviness of the piece suggesting it was Galen's, a worn but comfortable-looking sofa, a bar, a TV set, and a large box of toys. In one corner a stone hearth contained a fire that crackled merrily, in defiance of the storm that raged outside the windows.

'Will you come tell me goodnight when I'm in bed?' Billy asked her shyly.

Out of the corner of her eye she saw Galen's big frame stiffen, felt his eyes rest on her face. Obviously, the required answer, according to the lord of the manor, would be no.

'Of course I will,' she told Billy, partly to annoy Galen but mostly because she really wanted to.

Galen busied himself behind the bar, brought her a drink she hadn't asked for, and sank down in the overstuffed chair beside her.

She sipped the drink tentatively, and then sighed with contentment. Grand Marnier. A storm outside. A warm fire inside. It could have been a perfect romantic picture were it frozen in a photo in a

42

magazine, especially given his rugged good looks, his breathtaking build, the way he was leaning towards her intensely. But there was nothing romantic about the piercing gaze which was uncomfortably intent on her face, and her brief contentment gave way to tension.

'I'd rather you didn't work quite so hard at endearing yourself to my son.'

She gasped, and set down the glass with firm control, though a more wanton part of her dearly wanted to toss its contents at his haughty face.

'I haven't,' she informed him tightly, 'made any conscious effort to endear myself to Billy. It's true, I like him. And I'm flattered that he appears to like me. I don't see anything threatening about that.' In fact, the only threat she saw was gathering like storm clouds in his dark eyes.

'I just don't want the fact you're leaving tomorrow, and never coming back, to be too hard on him.'

'Don't be ridiculous,' she snapped. 'You're totally overreacting. Can you seriously think a friendship of a few hours is going to have any long-term effect on Billy, positive or negative? He's a child. He'll have forgotten my name by the end of next week.'

'Billy isn't like most kids.'

An unwanted smile broke through her irritation. 'You wouldn't be a father if you didn't believe that.'

He glowered at her, reminding her that he was a man who took himself altogether too seriously.

'My son is more tenacious than most children,' Galen informed her coldly. 'He sinks his little teeth into an idea, and becomes part bulldog. He won't let go until he gets what he wants.'

'I wonder where he got that charming quality from,' she mused innocently.

'When Billy was four years old, he decided he wanted a horse,' Galen continued, ignoring her comment. 'Not a pony, mind you, but a horse. Naturally, I thought it was a passing fancy, and that he'd forget about it when no horse was forthcoming, or at the very least scale his request down. A pony. A puppy.

'He got his horse when I couldn't stand his nagging any more. I held out for nearly two years, thinking he didn't know what he really wanted or what he was getting into. Two years of hearing the word horse almost every time he opened his mouth—which you may have noticed is frequently.' A sudden unguarded fondness leapt in Galen's eyes and his tone softened. 'Though I have to admit, I've been pleasantly surprised by his response to Sugar. We've had her nearly a year now, and his interest in her hasn't diminished a bit. He never forgets to look after her, and spends some time with her every day. I guess he knows his own mind.'

'Another quality that I just can't imagine where he came by,' Rae interjected wryly.

The unguarded softness left his voice, his face once again became remote. 'The point is, I'm hoping a ''mommy'' isn't the next campaign. And if it is, I can only hope ''mommy'' remains a vague unknown in his mind—someone that smells nice, and looks pretty and bakes cookies. In other words, I don't want his romantic notion to get your name attached to it, Ms Douglas.'

She could, unfortunately, see his point. There was no sense having the little boy decide she would be the perfect mommy for him, even though the thought of him driving Galen crazy was terribly tempting.

'I'll keep my goodnight as formal as I can without hurting his feelings,' she offered reluctantly.

Galen nodded moodily, took a long pull on his drink. 'Let's hope it's not too late. He's rather taken with you already.'

'Is he? I would have thought he was outgoing and friendly with everybody.'

'Oh, he is. But he misses Walt Disney for no one. He didn't even mention it tonight.'

'Oh, dear,' she murmured, 'a sign of undying devotion if I've ever heard one.'

Galen's glare clearly accused her of lacking perception in the true gravity of the matter. 'I just think it may indicate how high "mommy" is placed on the priority list.'

She felt a shaft of pity for Billy pierce her heart. Why he wanted a mother so desperately she didn't know. She only knew he did, and could remember from personal experience the anguish of childish longings going unanswered. Her own had been for a father, for a family. It was a longing that, buried, had grown in strength, blinding her to reality when Roger had come along.

'Isn't there any chance of you and his mother being reunited?' she queried softly.

'That isn't very likely,' Galen informed her with harsh humour, 'since his mother is dead.'

She noted his harshness. Was it Billy's mother, then, who had 'wounded' Galen? Who was responsible for the faint bitterness around that firm mouth? Who had robbed the laughter from those dark eyes?

'I'm sorry,' she said softly. 'I'm afraid I assumed

in this day and age that it would have been a divorce.'

'There are some things about this day and age I don't like very much,' Galen responded, 'and one of them is the light attitude taken toward marriage. The let's-try-it-on mentality—as if it were a pair of shoes.'

It was his second reference to shoes and marriage, and his opinion was obviously that anyone who shopped for a marriage by mail had no respect for that institution's sanctity.

'Mr MacNamara, I don't particularly appreciate your silently branding me an emotionally shallow, romantically fickle, hard and heartless person because I happened to answer your ad.'

'It wasn't my ad,' he pointed out calmly.

'All right, then! I still don't think you have the least right to sit in judgement. You don't understand. You don't know my motivations . . . and you don't know me!'

'Why *did* you answer that ad?' he asked, his tone amiable enough, though the look of hard censure never left his eyes.

Oh-oh! She'd walked herself right into that one. She was hardly going to come off in a better light if she admitted she'd answered the ad to flesh out a magazine article! That did seem like an inexcusably hard and heartless thing to do. Not that she cared what light he saw her in, she defended herself hotly. She was going to bat for the principle of the thing, for all the women who did choose this option in a hope of finding love and laughter and romance.

The women she'd talked to in the course of researching her article had not been fortune-hunters, had not been life's losers, had not been

timid wimps looking for a place to hide from life. If
anything, they had been women who still believed in
old-fashioned values: in love, and marriage and
children. Who believed in it, and yet had trouble
finding what they were looking for amid the plastic
faces and canned laughter of the singles scene.

Though Rae herself was embittered enough to
believe they were hopelessly naïve, she had given the
women her grudging respect, and, even now, was
willing to admit that some small part of her longed
for the same things they longed for. Love. Home.
Family. Were the words relics of another age? Did
the words represent an illusion, behind which lurked
the likes of Roger? She shuddered. Had Roger's
wife, the poor young thing, believed she had
attained all she had ever dreamed of?

'Rae, I'm ready.' The thin voice floated down to
the living-room, startling her out of an eerie world
suddenly inhabited by ghosts of the past, of her
dreams, of hope itself.

Galen was watching her closely—too closely—
making her feel her mind's tumult was an open book
to him. She rose hastily, but he rose too, blocking
her escape.

'Bily can wait a minute. Why?' he demanded
softly.

She looked up at him, aware of, appalled by the
yearning his solid strength stirred in her. Yes, his
face was hard, closed to her, but there was integrity
in those strong lines, too. This man would not play
cruel games with other people's hearts. Had she
recognised that as soon as she had seen his picture?

Why had she answered that ad? Because she was
researching an article, or because she wanted
revenge on the entire male species, to play her own

cruel game of hearts . . . or because a part of her had
hoped and longed for evidence that all that was good
was not dead? Perhaps a part of her had even hoped,
as soon as she had laid eyes on this man's picture,
that he would be the one. The one to lead her back to
a place of hope and dreams and love.

The unexpected discovery that she was still
capable of nourishing such fairy-tales at some deeply
subsconscious level was shattering—and just as
shattering was the realisation that he was *not* the one.
That here was a man who would not play games
with hearts, but who had placed his own heart off
limits to her. Without even knowing her. Without
wanting to know her. It hurt, as it had always hurt
when men didn't seem to find her attractive, and she
protected herself from the hurt by deciding she hated
him. And yet it seemed to be the hurt that he saw,
for faint concern furrowed his brow as he watched
her face.

'Rae——' He took a step towards her. Her name
sounded nice on his lips. It was an observation that
only unsettled her more. Unconsciously she backed
away from him, unaware that fear and
disillusionment had darkened her eyes to midnight
blue.

He stopped immediately, regarding her with a
frown. 'Are you all right, Rae?'

She wished he would stop using her name. She
wished she could summon the cold reserve to tell
him she preferred Ms Douglas. Instead she smiled
shakily. 'Of course. I'm fine,' she assured him with
tremulous blitheness. 'Could you tell me where
Billy's room is?'

His gaze stripped her bare and laid her heart and
soul before his sweeping eyes. He hesitated and then

shrugged, turning abruptly away from her.
Turning, she suspected, with her heart hammering
in her throat, from the impulse to get to know her
after all.

'Upstairs, second on the right.'

'Thank you.' She moved quickly away from him.
When she returned, they would move on to other
things, and her mind would have returned to
normal—rational, collected, analytical. Gone would
be the strange notion that a man who had never
shown her anything except hostility had been about
to sweep her into the comforting and powerful
embrace of his arms. Gone would be the notion that
she would have enjoyed that very much—because so
far, Galen MacNamara was not a man she liked in
the least. Why had some irrational part of her
emerged from behind the iron curtain of her control
to suggest she would enjoy the embrace of a man she
had just seconds ago resolved to hate?

The question was unsettling, and rather than deal
with it she hurried from the room and up the stairs,
determined that when she returned her rational self
would return with her.

Billy was sitting up in bed, looking deceptively
angelic in his cowboy-print pyjamas. His hair was
damp and curling, his face shiny-clean. His room,
she noticed, was any little boy's dream. The bed had
been built to resemble a fire engine, and was painted
brilliant red. Winnie the Pooh frolicked across one
wall; large, colourful wooden blocks that could
become a fortress or a train or any of a hundred
other things were stacked against another.

Galen MacNamara's mystery grew. Who was he?
A man hard, cold and bitter? But not all the way
through, not when he could be so gentle, so giving

with his son. Did only Billy realise Galen's tender side, his sensitive side? No. Because, for just a moment, he had almost shown it to her as well. Given time, would she see it again? A useless conjecture. There was no time. And in the short time there was, she would not let herself be vulnerable to him.

Without warning, the name Clarice popped into her head. Why did her heart sink at the thought that Galen might expose a warmer side to a woman she had never met? Why did an emotion that seemed dangerously close to envy swell up inside of her? Good grief, she didn't even like the man—why should she give two hoots about his tender side?

'Are you going to tell me a story?' Billy asked eagerly.

Rae turned her attention to him, regretfully remembering her promise to Galen. Perhaps Billy's interest in acquiring her as a mother would wane if she didn't have a good supply of stories.

'Not tonight,' she said vaguely, avoiding the lie that she didn't know any tales when in fact, when she was seeing Roger, she had secretly begun quite a collection of children's stories in wistful anticipation that one day they would have a family.

'Then I'll tell you one.' He slipped over in his bed, his dark eyes wide, trusting and inviting on her face.

She knew she should say she had just come to say goodnight, and yet she couldn't. Her legs carried her over to the bed, and she sat down. A small hand crept into hers, and Billy launched himself into a wildly rambling original creation that involved spacemen and Mars and a lost dog.

She looked down at him, steadfastly resisting the

impulse to ruffle his hair, to put her arm around him
and encourage him to snuggle into her. She felt a
lump tightening in her throat, and again, she was
threatened by the ghosts that she had worked so hard
and long to outrun.

How many dreamy evenings had she spent while
she was seeing Roger planning their cosy little
family? Evenings that he had claimed took him out
of town on business, when in actual fact he was at
home with a wife? Evenings wasted on speculating
what their children would look like, imagining
moments so much like this one.

Billy's voice had grown husky, and then it stopped
and his head dropped against her breast. Gently,
aware of tears stinging behind her eyes, she tucked
him in and tiptoed from the room. Yes, it was a good
thing she was leaving tomorrow. Her heart was
closed to Galen MacNamara, and his to her, but this
little boy was breaking through the sinewy barriers
of scar-tissue that Roger had left. This little boy was
making her want to love again. And that was
dangerous. Loving had nearly destroyed her the first
time around. She wasn't strong enough to play that
game again. And she wasn't naïve enough to believe
in happily-ever-after endings.

Gramps was down the hall as she was returning to
the stairs.

'Bedtime for this old codger,' he said, yawning
heartily. She shook her head wryly. Gramps should
be in line for an Academy Award for all his
performances today.

'You might as well stay up,' she told him. 'Not a
single thing will come of your plotting for us to be
alone together.'

He only gave her a petulant look, sighed, and

continued on his way.

Galen was at the window, scowling furiously out into the swirling snow as if the force of his will could bring the raging storm to a skidding halt. He turned as she sank back down into a large chair and retrieved her Grand Marnier.

'I'm afraid Billy is very hard to be formal with,' she said defensively, though he had made no reference to the length of her stay in his son's room.

Galen nodded curtly, then came and lowered himself in the large chair next to hers. His leg brushed hers for a lengthy moment—heat and raw strength radiating from it. To her discredit, she waited longer than she had to to break away from the contact.

'You were just telling me why you answered the ad,' he said silkily, his gaze half-lidded, unintentionally sensual, and yet headily sensual all the same. Her eyes moved of their own will to the firm line of his lips, and a surge of pure and animal wanting raced red-hot through her veins. After her dreary days of half-life the sensation was shocking—delicious, but shocking. Never had her blood been stirred to race through her veins like liquid flame by a gesture so tiny as her eyes inadvertently catching on a set of lips.

She had always considered herself a more intellectual than physical person. She was not given to raging desires—and she had used this self-knowledge to explain away the fact that Roger's kisses and embraces had not left her aching for more. In the end, it had saved her sanity that she had never given into his pressure for the relationship to deepen into physical intimacy. When they were married, she had thought reasonably, feeling a pleasant anticipation. But now she was aware that some things were without reason. Now she knew she had not loved Roger, so much as loved what love stood for. For the first time she felt relief instead of agony at her near miss. But at the same time she had to acknowledge that she was capable of being blinded by her emotions. And maybe it was already happening again. Maybe she was already seeing strength where there was really weakness, the capacity for tenderness where there was none . . . maybe she was already seeing exactly what she wanted to see, and not the truth. How could she ever know again what was real and what was the distortion of a lonely soul, and a secretly romantic mind?

Galen cleared his throat. 'The ad?' he pressed.

'I'm not sure why I answered it,' she admitted uneasily. That, at least, was true.

His dark brows furrowed, and his eyes scanned her face relentlessly. Unsettled, she turned her profile from him, looking out of the window into the storm.

A strong hand reached out, and a finger touched her chin, feather-soft and yet demanding. Rae turned back and regarded him with wide eyes.

'You're an attractive woman, Rae. Something doesn't ring true about your searching through the want ads for a husband. I would think the eligible swains would be lining up at your door.'

'You would think wrong,' she said, attempting to keep her voice light. In fact, she spoke the truth again. The mirror told her she was reasonably if not earth-stoppingly attractive. And yet she had never been successful with men. In high school, in college, later with the after-work crowd, she'd attended dances and functions. All around her people were asked to dance, or sought out by strangers for conversation, but rarely did this happen to her. Perhaps, because she had never had a male influence in her life, she simply had never learned to throw out the right signals. Her mother was a serious intellectual—a professor at the University of Calgary. She hadn't had time for men in her life—she barely had time for her daughter. So it stood to reason that she definitely had had neither the time nor the patience to teach her daughter a few feminine skills.

A high-school girlfriend had told her she came across as too haughty in her encounters with men. In fact, the veneer of reserve hid an almost crippling shyness. In college, an old professor had taken a liking to her and informed her confidentially that through he immensely enjoyed her keen intellect, he feared most members of his sex would find her a trifle intimidating. And then Sal, watching her rise steadily through the ranks of *Womanworld*, had told her success wouldn't bode well if she ever wanted to find a husband.

Which she had denied heartily that she ever wanted to do. It wasn't fashionable to want a husband or marriage. She'd been raised with philosophies of liberation and independence. A career was expected of her. She had long since choked back the old-fashioned longings that had haunted her childhood. Forgotten them. Dismissed them as foolish.

Besides, she had never been able to attract male interest. And she loved her job. She didn't consciously resent her fate of being single—in fact, she'd enjoyed her solitude, her independence, her freedom. Or so she'd thought. Why, then, had she been so ripe for Roger's attentions? She had fallen with a thud with barely a nudge from him. Maybe he was the first person who had ever tried to reach behind the mask she bravely wore for the world. Or in retrospect, maybe he was a hunter, adept at picking out the weak and the vulnerable. Adept at spotting those who hungered for love, and hid their hunger behind façades of reserve and career interest.

Looking back, the situation had been humiliating. She had performed with the eagerness of a trained seal for the titbits of attention and affection he threw her. She had made excuses for his faults, rationalised the gaps in their relationship. She had always assumed she knew his heart—therefore it had never occurred to her to confirm what he thought the relationship meant, where he thought it was going. He'd said he loved her—she assumed that meant he would one day marry her—though he never mentioned it, and she never pressed. She must have known there were office parties and functions of Roger's that she was never asked to attend, and yet it was a knowledge she had hidden from, engrossed as she had been in a fantasy world with a fantasy prince. And then that world had exploded in her face——

'If that's part of the act, you can drop it.'

'The act?' she looked at Galen with startled surprise.

'That look that comes into your eyes—a haunted and hurt look that's probably lured many a man to his downfall. It won't work on me. Get it through your head that I am not in the market for a wife, and that you're leaving as soon as it can be humanly arranged.'

She could feel herself beginning to tremble with rage. Part of it was caused by the unabashed arrogance of the man, and part from being caught licking her wounds—and then being accused of being a fraud on top of it!

'Why did you answer that ad?' he mocked. 'Did you manage to get a hold of my financial statement?'

'Mr MacNamara, I told you I don't really know why I answered that ad. But I knew the moment I laid eyes on you this afternoon that it was the biggest mistake of my existence. You are a boor beyond belief. You are rude, insufferable, and insensitive. You are . . . are as sour as month-old milk! As for your financial statement, I wouldn't care if you were worth a billion dollars. I wouldn't marry you if you were the last man on earth——' the amusement that danced openly and wickedly in his eyes fuelled the flame of her anger, and her voice rose recklessly '—I wouldn't even stay in your house tonight if I could think of a way not to. Believe me, no one will be happier than me to get out of here tomorrow, though I don't think I can tolerate the thought of your company on a long drive. Gramps can drive me. I'll take a bus. I'll walk! I'll——'

A sudden thundering crash ripped through her tirade. Both her and Galen jumped from their seats and looked out into the murky darkness where the explosive, deafening sound had come from.

Suddenly understanding lit Galen's face, and he shook his head slowly. 'I don't believe it.' He cursed softly under his breath.

'What? What was it?'

He gave her his full attention, his look a curious

mix of anger and disbelief.

'It was the bridge,' he informed her quietly.

'The bridge?' she echoed stupidly.

'Yes. You know—the bridge you have to cross to get on to this side of the river. I'd say it's gone.'

She stared at him blankly. 'Well, surely that isn't the only way——'

'The only way.'

'When do you accuse me of dynamiting it?' she asked acidly.

His eyebrows rose sardonically. 'After the little speech I just heard? Do I look like a man who would take his life in his hands?' He turned back to the window, his expression black. 'They couldn't have arranged it,' he muttered. 'How could they have arranged it?'

'How long——'

'I don't know,' he snapped, then his tone relaxed slightly. 'A week, maybe. Maybe a little more.'

'I can't stay here a week! I have a job to think about.'

He turned and gave her a look of mild interest. 'A job? That makes me even more curious about the search for a husband. Unless the tedium of work is what you're trying to escape. What do you do?'

'I sell shoes,' she fired back sarcastically.

'Farm wives do not live a life of ease,' he informed her. 'They work damn hard. Maybe it won't be so bad for you to be forced to stay here a few days and learn what's involved in being a farm woman. You might not be so eager to run back to the city and start shopping through more ads placed by lonely farmers.'

'It seems to me maybe we should call some sort of truce if we're going to be forced to spend a week under the same roof.' Her façade of reasonableness made her feel smugly superior—even if the truth was she would have liked to smack his arrogant handsome face with all her might.

'A truce it is,' he agreed coolly. 'And these are the conditions. Stay the hell out of my way. And my son's.'

She stared at him, hating him. She had extended the hand of peace, and he had declared war. But hating him, too, because his lips beckoned hers like the ghost lighthouses of legend beckoned ships.

'Show me my room,' she demanded coldly.

'I mean it, Rae. Don't try to get to me through my son. Don't use him.'

'I already told you how I feel about you as husband material,' she reminded him hotly, feeling stung that he would think her capable of doing anything so low. Then she wondered, with shame, if her thoughts of his lips for a few seconds ago might have been horribly obvious, if something in her eyes had given the lie to her words of contempt.

'Just show me my room,' she pleaded, suddenly weary, confused and troubled.

'That look is in your eyes again.' The hard edge was gone from his voice, a look of faint puzzlement softening the pitch of his eyes. And then all his hardness was back, stronger than before. 'As I said, just stay out of my way.'

She knew, then, with that deep knowing that was often called a woman's intuition, that he had been a second away from kissing her. The hair on the back of her neck bristled, her heart flip-flopped crazily inside her.

Yes, she would stay out of his way. For her sake, not his. But how? Good lord, how?

CHAPTER FOUR

THE bedroom was lovely. It had a sloped, open-beam ceiling, golden log walls, dark, polished hardwood floors brightened with scatter rugs. At one end was a large bowed window, with a built-in window-seat tucked in its nook. At the other end was a door through which Rae could glimpse a tiny bathroom. An antique four-poster bed and matching bureau completed the room.

It was a peaceful place, and she flopped on the bed and felt the beat of her heart return slowly to normal. Had Galen designed this room? She suspected he had, just as she suspected his influence was the major one in the design of the whole house. There was something about these solid, warm rooms that marked them irrevocably as his. And yet she had to wonder what would make her draw that conclusion. The face he showed the world—or more appropriately, the face he had shown her—was hard and cold and stern. Not the face of a man who could generate such a feeling of warmth with the use of wood and light and space.

Who was Galen MacNamara? He was definitely about the most confusing man she had ever met. He was a man who could be cold and insensitive to the point of rudeness. He was also the man whose dark eyes deepened with the most exquisite tenderness when he looked at his son. One moment cynical, the next compassionate; one moment good-humoured, the next aloof.

The key to his mystery, she mused, lay somewhere in the depths of those dark eyes. The secret self that flashed through though he tried to hide it; the self that showed in these rooms and in the looks of unguarded affection he gave his son. His eyes were three-tiered, as he was. There was that cold, haughtily aloof part, and then the wall—the barrier left by some unspeakable wound—and then something beyond. A garden of good earth and blossoms that only slept, that had not been destroyed by winter . . .

She scowled thoughtfully. Even without Gramps' warning, she would have known, intuitively, that this man had been wounded. By what? By whom? Was it Billy's mother who had left these scars? Were they permanent?

Rae sat up abruptly and cursed herself soundly. It was re-emerging—that quality Sal referred to as her tender touch. Her foolish, romantic notions, her desire to see beyond the face and touch the soul. It was a quality that had got her into trouble before—her tenderness and her imagination teaming up to build her a man who had never existed.

And yet she could not shake a quote that insisted on running through her head. 'What is essential is invisible to the eye.' And then she remembered it came from one of her favourite books, *The Little Prince*.

'Dear God,' she muttered, 'release me from the bondage of fairy-tales.' And yet her eyes wandered around the room again, and she repeated the phrase.

It was true. What was essential about this room—and this man—was indeed invisible to the

eye. It was that intangible thing called human spirit
that she sensed. That thing that remained unscarred
and unscathed in the deepest part of all men, despite
their trials and tribulations—waiting for the smallest
hint of sunshine to heal it and help it burst through
again. And she could sense his here, in this room, and
sense it in him, even though he kept it so leashed.
Something strong, sensitive, good.

'Ha!' she berated herself, annoyed that her thoughts
had once again run amok without her consent. Had
she learned nothing from Roger? She must believe
only what Galen showed her—not what she wanted to
believe, or even suspected to be true. Truth was that
black and white stuff that you could touch and
see—not the wild conjecturings of a wayward mind.

She got ready for bed, and moments later slipped
between fresh-smelling sheets. She took up the
shorthand pad she used for notes, and began to make
some thumbnail sketches—with words—of her first
impressions of the farm. She didn't know why. The
article was doomed. And yet she felt driven to capture
the little of it she had experienced. The fresh, clean
tang of the air when she had first stepped from the car,
the lowing of cattle that provided background music to
dinner, and the exquisite warmth this house radiated.

Finally, she switched off the light and lay in
absolute darkness, listening to absolute silence.
Well, not really silence—the wind still howled
relentlessly. And yet the sound was so pure,
unbroken by car tyres screaming, by the sounds of
people walking and laughing, unbroken by the
sounds of water running in the apartment next door,
or heavy footsteps overhead.

She was momentarily tempted to turn the light
back on and make a few additional notes, but found

herself too weary. She had thought she would be
awake most of the night contemplating the near miss
of Galen's kiss. Turning him inside and out in her
mind, trying to understand him. Turning herself
inside and out, looking for what was real, in a world
she could no longer trust.

But instead, she fell asleep, almost instantly, to
the symphony of a raging wind.

Rae awoke to the sound of boyish laughter. The grey
light of pre-dawn washed her room. A wintry chill
permeated the air and she nestled deeper under her
quilt. It was damned cold, it was an ungodly hour,
and she lay listening grouchily to the chirping of
Billy in the room next door, hoping someone would
send the irrepressible child back to bed. He could be
irrepressible at a decent hour, surely?

Slowly her grumpiness dissolved. The room next
door, she realised, must be Galen's, because the low
rumble of his laughter had joined Billy's squealing.
She shut her eyes, and could picture them wrestling
playfully among tumbled sheets. It was the kind of
childhood experience that she had never had, and
yet had known existed, and had longed for. Even
now she felt a funny, stabbing aching inside her, a
craving to be part of their fun, to belong.

'Hush up, you two! Ain't ya got no manners?
We've got a guest.' Gramps' voice entering the
mêlée brought the smile back to Rae's lips.

There was a momentary silence, and then Billy
asked in a whisper that no doubt carried to the barn,
'Does that mean we can't have our Sunday parade
this morning?'

'Of course not,' she heard Galen respond, and an
outlaw vision of his broad and naked chest invaded

her mind. 'Gramps, it won't hurt her to find out that there's more to being a farm woman than vacationing in Phoenix for the winter.'

Rae pursed her lips indignantly. She happened to know there was more to it than that. Her mental meanderings about this man last night must have been caused by a dose of unbelievable weariness!

The three voices faded, followed by other wake-up noises—most notably the sound of a shower running in the room adjoining hers. Once again a renegade vision insisted on popping into her head. She buried her head under the pillow, doing her best not to admit that she was now well and truly awake.

The shower sounds stopped, and were followed by a crash that sent her bolting upright to a sitting position. The sound repeated and picked up something that approximated rhythm. A pot and spoon drum, she guessed, uncertain whether to laugh or scream. She peered at her watch in the muted light of barely morning. It was hardly past five. And yet a delighted chuckle slipped by her unwilling lips anyway. They had started to sing. Billy's voice, high and definitely out of tune, led the way.

'Oh, my name is MacNamara . . .'

Gramps, as badly out of tune as Billy, but none the less enthusiastic, joined in.

'. . . and I'm the leader of the band . . .'

And then Galen's voice, deep and sure, if not exactly melodious, joined the other two.

'. . . 'tis the finest band in all of Ireland . . .'

Stamping their feet in a deafening march, they wove through the house and down the stairs, their voices finally fading as they entered the kitchen.

Their morning ritual, she thought with a surprised grin. Somehow she would have never guessed from Galen's picture, or from the way he had treated her, that he had a deeply rooted sense of fun. Or maybe that wasn't completely true. Maybe that sense of fun, or joy, was part of what she had sensed but not seen. Perhaps her intuition wasn't so darned untrustworthy, after all . . .

She lingered determinedly in bed. She was certain Galen's remarks about there being more to being a farm woman than spending the winters in Phoenix had been deliberately voiced loudly enough for her to hear—and she was damned if she was going to entertain him by doing backflips to try and win his approval. He no doubt thought his loud hint would bring her cascading down the stairs, bright-eyed and bushy-tailed, and falling all over herself to cook the menfolk breakfast. He hadn't seemed entirely convinced last night, even with her vehemence, that she wasn't the slightest bit interested in him as a partner in matrimony. Maybe ignoring his hint and sleeping till ten would convince him of her sincerity.

She was surprised, however, when she couldn't will herself back to sleep. She was no morning person—the last time she had seen five a.m. was in those nightmarish weeks after Roger's betrayal. And then it was from lying awake for entire nights, pondering, reliving, questioning, screaming silently the eternal 'Why?'.

Warmth crept into her room, but it was the smell of frying bacon that drove her from her bed, into the shower, and down the stairs. She noted only briefly that her clothing supply was not going to last a

week, and hoped that Galen had been overly
pessimistic about when the bridge would be fixed.

It turned out he had been overly optimistic. He
was on the phone when she entered the kitchen.

'Come on, Ralph, you can do better than that.'

His back was to her, but as she sat at the table she
couldn't resist the occasional furtive glance in his
direction. Somehow over the space of the night she
had forgotten how tremendously big and well-
proportioned he was, forgotten how overwhelming
his presence in a room could be. Was it her
imagination, or over the smell of bacon could she
make out the faint aroma of aftershave, as clean and
fresh as sun warming the earth?

'Two weeks?' Galen roared. 'Ralph, damn
it——' He stopped, and listened, his broad
shoulders suddenly lowered in resignation. 'Yeah,
we're OK for food and feed. No, no, we won't need
a chopper drop.' He turned suddenly and looked
right at her, making her aware that he had known
the moment she walked in the room. 'We won't
need a helicopter yet,' he said softly, his gaze resting
on her face, 'though I'll let you know if I reach the
end of my rope. But it would be something going
out, not coming in.' He slammed down the receiver
and marched out the door, letting it slam behind him
as well.

Rae gave in to the childish urge to stick out her
tongue at his departing back. Could this obnoxious
excuse for a human being be the same one who had
marched around the house singing cheerfully this
morning?

'OK, Gramps, how'd you do it?' she demanded.

'Do what?' he asked innocently, proudly placing a
plate of flapjacks and bacon and eggs in front of her.

'How did you get rid of the bridge?' she persisted.

'Don't be silly,' he admonished her indignantly. 'I didn't get rid of the bridge. Jeez, between you and Galen, a man can't get no peace. He woke me up out of a dead sleep last night askin' the same foolish question.'

'The circumstances seem to warrant a bit of suspicion,' she told him, straight-faced.

'I didn't do nothing to the bridge. I bet Galen's out there looking for evidence of that right now, desrespectful young pup that he is. But that bridge does have a habit of going 'bout every nine years or so, and I have a pal that works in the weather department . . .'

'Even so, you couldn't possibly have known a day, a time . . .'

'That's true, and you can tell that to my son,' Gramps agreed placidly, sliding into the chair across from her and fixing her with merry blue eyes. 'I just knew that Billy and I could do our parts, but if it were meant to be, destiny would have to play its part, too.'

For a moment she was tempted to laugh, but the expression on Gramps' face stopped her. Why, the old fool was deadly serious!

'Gramps,' she said carefully, 'it was a coincidence. I don't think it would be wise for you to decide that because the bridge went, a romance between Galen and I has been appointed by the stars. And I don't think it would be wise to encourage Billy to believe that.'

'Now, look here, missy,' he responded patiently, as if he were explaining a difficult concept to a dull child, 'I been around a good deal longer than you, and I can tell you this—there ain't no such thing as

coincidence. Things happen because that's what
people need to learn—because they're supposed to
happen. I ain't saying where these two weeks will
lead, I'm just saying they was meant to be.'

With a little nudge from you they were meant to
be, she responded silently, and couldn't prevent
herself from smiling at the look of certainty on his
face.

Galen returned a few minutes later, and gave
Gramps a glowering look that said his inspection of
the remains of the bridge had turned up nothing, but
Gramps was still not off the hook.

They sat down to an enormous farm-style
breakfast.

'Did you call Clarice?' Galen asked Gramps, and
though Rae did not look up from her laden plate she
felt herself stiffen with curiosity.

'Nah. Didn't figure a little stretch of water would
mean beans to a barracuda.'

Galen sighed with irritation. 'Look, she's stuck
over here, the same as us. Would you please do her
the courtesy of letting her know, instead of her
having to drive down and find out herself?'

'You let her know,' Gramps returned stubbornly,
but Rae was busy digesting the fact that
Clarice—why on earth did she think of her as her
competition?—was on this side of the river.

'Clarice lives over here?' she asked casually.

'Farm's just down the road a bit,' Galen said.

Rae shot Gramps a puzzled look. His plan made
less and less sense. Obviously she and Galen were
not gong to be stranded together in isolation. And
obviously Clarice was a better choice for him as a
mate. A farmer. They would have a great deal in
common. Not that she cared, she told herself firmly.

'I have to make a phone call myself,' she said. 'I'll be expected at work on Monday.'

'Ah, yes,' Galen said smoothly. 'The shoe store.'

'Actually, I work in the advertising department of a magazine.' She had devised this story even before she had answered his ad. She had worked in *Womanworld's* advertising department for a short time. And it was close enough to the truth that she wasn't likely to trip herself up. Why did the little lie make her feel so guilty? It was a legitimate part of a reporter's job to go undercover to get a good story. She had once worked as a waitress in a cocktail lounge to that end. She had taken police training to get an article on women in the force. She had done things like this dozens of times. Sort of like this. So why did it feel so different this time? Underhanded, sneaky, unethical? She dismissed the thoughts, or tried to dismiss them. She was just doing her job, after all.

'And so,' she finished telling Sal over the phone, 'it looks as if I'll be stuck here for two weeks.'

'That might not be so bad. Come on, kid, you're holding out. What's he like?'

'Billy or Gramps?' she asked with feigned innocence.

'Ha! You're pretending he doesn't exist. That's a dead giveaway. He's awesome, isn't he?'

'Who?' Rae insisted stubbornly.

'Give it up. This is old Sal you're talking to. The Celtic chieftain, that's who.'

'Oh,' Rae said weakly, 'him.' She contemplated the question for a moment. 'Sal, I guess I don't honestly know. He's as cool as a wind from the Arctic most of the time, but occasionally a bit

of sun shines through, mostly just for Billy.' She
decided not to confide in her boss how unbearably
attractive he was in those brief moments. 'Besides, it
doesn't matter. As I told you, I think I was brought
here by Gramps and Billy to throw a wrench in a
romance that may be progressing towards the
serious.'

'Oh, I don't know. I'll play the long shot and side
with Gramps. Destiny had a hand in this.'

'Don't be ridiculous,' Rae said sharply. 'Besides,
the woman he's interested in lives on this side of the
bridge, as well.'

'Does she? This gets more interesting by the
moment. Anyway, if I can't be ridiculous, let's talk
business. Obviously the prospective-bride angle for
the story has been blown to smithereens. But maybe
we can salvage something.'

There was a silence of a few seconds and Rae
explored the den with her eyes, searching a shelf of
photographs for a picture of the mystery Clarice, or
Galen's dead wife. The pictures were plentiful—of
Billy and Gramps and an assortment of animals.
Not a single woman. For some reason that reassured
her—maybe it wasn't just her he hated—maybe it
was her entire gender. She scowled. So how had
Clarice slipped by his guard and won his trust,
particularly in light of Billy's and Gramps' dis-
like?

'I've got it!' Sal crowed. 'Rae, most of our
readers are fairly sophisticated, urban women. Let's
just tell them what they'd be in for if they answered
one of those ads. What would be involved in
adapting to a country life-style. So get out there and
hoe a few rows and milk a few cows—not to mention
milking Mr MacNamara junior, for vital and excit-

ing information about farming. Do whatever it is a
farm wife would do.'

'Spend the winter in Phoenix,' Rae muttered,
Galen's warning to stay out of his way making her
wonder if Sal wasn't asking the impossible.

'What?'

'Nothing.'

'OK. See you in a couple of weeks.' She paused.
'And for Pete's sake, Rae, have fun.'

'You know, I think I will,' Rae responded. In
fact, she couldn't think of anything that sounded
more fun than antagonising Galen. And she
couldn't think of anything that would antagonise
him more than her being underfoot all the time,
insisting that he teach her everything that there was
to know about being a farm woman—supposedly so
that she could make a better impression when she
answered her next ad. How dared he order her to
stay out of his way, anyway?

'Sal, I might be back sooner—if he orders a
helicopter.'

'Why on earth would he go to the trouble and
expense of doing that?'

'I wouldn't know,' Rae responded sweetly, and
hung up.

Billy was waiting impatiently for her. 'Boy, girls
jabber a lot,' he pouted.

'Look who's talking,' she shot back.

He grinned at her. 'Want to see the farm now?'

She hesitated. Galen's warning had included his
son, but how on earth could she realistically stay
away from either of them, short of locking herself in
her room for the duration? Perhaps this would be a
very good opportunity to set things straight in Billy's
mind. She could not give in to the temptation to

have him drive Galen crazy by seeing her as a
mother-figure. Because his feelings were at stake,
and she felt a tremendous responsibility to his
feelings. That meant she would have to douse the
expectations Gramps had been so busily building.
She would not hurt this little child—not for an
article, not for anything on the earth.

'Sure,' she said, 'Let's go see the farm.' His
hand nestled in hers and he tugged her out the
door.

The tree-house was the first stop, and she could
see Galen's hand in its construction. It was a
lovely little fortress for a small boy's adven-
tures.

Rae looked out over the view it offered, and then
sank down on to a little wooden bench built into one
corner.

'Billy, you and I need to talk for a minute.'

'About what?' he said, hopping up and down at
the railing.

'I think it's very important that you understand
I'm not going to be your mother.'

His face fell. 'Yes, you are. Because the bridge fell
down and everything.'

Oh, Gramps, she thought dejectedly. 'Billy, it
doesn't have anything to do with the bridge. It has a
great deal to do with your father. He has the right to
choose his own wife. It must be someone who he
feels he has something in common with, somebody
he likes immensely and enjoys being with——'

'Aw, Rae, he likes you,' Billy said doubtfully.

'About as much as you like carrots. Billy, how
would you like it if somebody tried to force you to eat
carrots? Tried to insist you liked them when you
didn't?'

'I wouldn't like that very much,' Billy conceded reluctantly.

'Then maybe it would be better if you didn't try to force me on your dad. I noticed he respected your choice, about not eating carrots. Now you have to do the same for him, about me.'

'But I like you,' Billy said stubbornly.

'And that's good, and I'm very, very glad, because I like you, too. You know, we can be friends. You can choose me as a friend for yourself—but not for your father.'

'Oh,' Billy said in a small voice, then, 'Don't you like my dad?'

Oh, dear, how to tell a small boy that the man he worshipped was an obnoxious boor? No, she wouldn't say that anyway, because a part of her didn't believe Galen was like that through and through.

'I think,' she said cautiously, 'that your father is a fine man.' True. A good father, a hard worker, a hint of creativity and sensitivity about him. 'But I don't think he's the type I would ever marry.' Actually, for some reason, she didn't believe that quite as strongly, but she reminded herself sternly that the point of this conversation was to convince Billy that nothing, but nothing, was ever going to occur between her and his father. Which it wasn't, regardless of the fact that she found Galen almost unsettlingly attractive and intriguing.

'We can be friends,' she repeated firmly. 'Having a friend is a wonderful thing—just about the best in the world.'

'But having a mom would be better.'

She nodded gravely. 'I suppose it would be. But since you can't have that from me, would you settle for having me as a friend?'

Billy studied his sneakers, and finally looked up. 'I guess so.' He gave her a tentative smile. 'Do friends ever bake chocolate chip cookies for each other?'

'It has been known to happen,' she responded solemnly.

'OK.' He headed for the ladder. 'I'll race you to the barn, pal.'

CHAPTER FIVE

GALEN was crouched over a sick cow in the barn when the door crashed open, and Billy and Rae came in, laughter ringing in the air between them. Although he stood up, he knew he was swathed in shadows and he made no move to let them know he was there.

His eyes narrowed wrathfully at the woman whose arm was slung so casually over his son's shoulder. He clenched and unclenched a fist. Damn it. He had asked her to stay away from Billy. No, he admitted, backing down a little. He hadn't asked. He had ordered. He suspected that was like waving a red flag in front of his unwanted guest.

He studied her, not liking what he saw. Or, more aptly, not liking the faint stirring within him. Her short hair was wind-ruffled, her cheeks high with colour, those enormous sad serious eyes made rather wondrous by laughter. She was an attractive woman, he admitted grudgingly. Not beautiful, not glamorous, and yet nice-looking, in a natural kind of way.

He snorted impatiently to himself. Natural. Oh, no. He wouldn't walk into that trap again. He knew all about city women, and their contrived ways. If she looked natural, it was no doubt because she had worked long and hard to look that way.

She took a deep breath of odour-laden air, but he was rather surprised to see that she looked appreci-

ative rather than disgusted. He had not expected her
to share his enjoyment of the earthy, tart barn
smells, and it annoyed him that she seemed to. He
shored up his cynicism by noticing that she was
mud-spattered up to the knee of her camel-coloured
denims, and that her shoes were caked in black.
Hadn't even had the sense to put on a pair of
gumboots, he thought, not without satisfaction. And
she thought she wanted to marry a farmer. She
didn't know the first thing about farming or farmers,
and he wondered, again, what her motive was.

Billy was tugging her towards the horse stall, and
she jumped back when Sugar's huge white head
popped over the railing of her box stall, and swung
around to regard her. Billy laughed at her
reluctance. 'This is Sugar. Come and pet her. She's
gentle as a kitten.'

'And big as a moose,' Rae blurted out, her
wariness evident in the stiffened line of her body.
'You know, Billy, I once had to go to hospital for
stitches because a "gentle" kitten ripped open my
arm.'

Billy rolled his eyes. So did Galen.

Rae edged a touch closer to the horse, evidently
ready to bolt. Galen wished the horse would snort.

'Hold out your hand,' Billy encouraged.

Taking a deep breath, she closed her eyes and
held out her hand. Then she was butted gently with
a muzzle, and Galen waited smugly for the scream.
Instead he heard her laugh with soft delight.

'She wants you to pet her,' Billy interpreted
officiously.

Rae moved closer, her childlike sense of wonder
glowing in widened eyes. Tentatively she rubbed the
horse's forehead, and was rewarded with a faint

whicker, a sigh of pleasure, and closed eyes.

Galen felt his interest stir again at her look of unbridled enthusiasm as she stroked the horse, her features soft and gentle, unguarded, lacking the look of controlled sophistication he had noticed yesterday. Her eyes were finally free of that look of sadness that seemed to lurk about her.

He crushed his feelings of empathy and interest savagely. He'd walked through that barn door with another woman years ago. Proudly showing off what was his to his new bride. She had been a city woman, too.

'Galen,' she'd shrieked girlishly, 'it stinks!'

He sniffed the air now. No, it didn't stink. It smelled, but it smelled of good things—hay and horses and cattle. And it had not offended Rae's citified senses.

He shrank further back in the shadows as they came towards him, but they stopped at Bossy, the milk cow's stall.

'But isn't that a bull?' Rae asked nervously, once again holding back.

Billy hooted with derision, and Galen had to stifle his own shout of laughter. City girl, he thought again, trying hard to feel contempt, and smiling all the same.

'Well, it—I mean, she—has horns,' Rae told Billy defensively. 'I thought only bulls had horns.'

Galen's smile deepened, and he watched as once again she fought down her fear, and then it melted into an expression of wonder and delight that made her incredibly beautiful, erased completely that world-weary and haunted expression from her face. He wondered what had put that expression there, then forced himself to stop wondering. He didn't

want to know. He didn't want to know anything
about her.

So why then did he feel compelled to follow them
when they went up to the loft to look at the kittens?
The opening where the ladder went into the loft was
as shadowed as the stall had been, and again he
watched them unnoticed.

Rae was snuggling up comfortably in a deep pile
of hay, kittens crawling all over her. She was
laughing softly, and held one to her bosom tenderly,
her fingers playing lightly with his ears. Obviously
not too concerned about being scratched, despite her
claim that a kitten had once sent her to the hospital.

Again he felt a ghost. Another woman sitting in
the hay. 'Galen, it scratches,' she'd pouted. Had
there been kittens then?

An unwanted memory crashed in around him. He
was holding the baby to her. Billy, so tiny, so
helpless, mewing like a kitten. She had turned her
face away, her indifference cutting through him like
a knife.

'Ugly, wrinkled little monster,' she had stated
with a flat lack of emotion. Less tenderness for her
own son than this woman had for a kitten.

He felt again the helpless anger, found himself
regarding Rae suspiciously. They all seemed to be
something they weren't—until you brought them
home. Sara, too, had seemed tender and gentle and
loving. An act. An act that hid an emptiness and a
restlessness—one he could not fill, the other he could
not heal.

And Gramps wondered why he liked Clarice.
Gramps saw her as hard as nails, but what he saw
was a woman who was frank and businesslike,
devoid of cutesy artifices. With Clarice there were

no twittering little smiles to disguise a heart of stone,
a soul of ice.

It had been several months now since she had
suggested they get married, a conversation he now
suspected Billy had overheard.

He'd been surprised, and then felt betrayed. 'I
suppose now you're going to tell me you love me,'
he'd said cynically.

She'd laughed. 'Don't be ridiculous. Love is for
teenagers who want to carve their names on trees.
What I had in mind was a partnership of equals.'
She'd touched his cheek with naked promise. 'With
a few physical perks thrown in for icing.'

He had thought about it off and on. Marrying
Clarice made sense. They came from the same rural
background. They shared the same all-consuming
interest—their farms. She had a keen intellect; he
enjoyed her company. The business aspect was
lucrative—the joining of two large, profitable farms.
Besides, she wouldn't kill him with cloying
dependency. But, for all the sense it made, there was
a reluctance in him that he could not bring himself to
probe. She didn't mention marriage again. Neither
did he.

'Dad! What are you doing there?'

Reluctantly he hoisted himself into the loft. 'Er—I
heard you.' I was spying, he thought with
astonishment.

'Galen, take this one. It looks just like you.'

Rae was beside him, looking up at him with
laughter-filled eyes, holding a bright carrot-
coloured kitten with a rather scowling demeanour up
to him.

She smelled of wild flowers, he thought. Wild

flowers and crushed hay. It was this second scent
that made a forbidden picture leap lightning swift
through his mind. Of her pressed into the hay
beneath him, of him covering her face with tender
kisses.

He turned abruptly from her, discomforted that
any woman could elicit that kind of response from
him. Maybe boys entertained such silly, fantastic
notions—but men? He knew Sara would have found
the notion repugnant. She had definitely been the
silk sheets and champagne type, now that he thought
about it, which he hadn't done before.

And her, this woman who stood before him? He
gave himself a mental shake. Romps in the hay
didn't happen in real life—and in real life, romps of
any kind had a price tag. She had already, from the
look in her eyes, paid some fearful price for
something. Well, so had he.

He had Gramps. He had Billy. He had his farm.
It was enough. It had been enough for a long, long
time. The fact that she didn't have even that wasn't
his fault, his responsibility. He crushed the ache that
the thought of her loneliness created inside him,
reminded himself brutally that women were as much
illusion as anything else. Was she really lonely,
or did she just want her winters in Phoenix, after
all?

He refused the kitten with a tight, 'No, thanks.'
She pulled it back, tucked it close against her breast,
her eyes on him wide and bewildered. Hurt. The
expression made him want to apologise—or worse,
to go and take the proffered kitten from her and give
himself over to the laughter that shimmered in the
air between her and Billy. But no, in its own way
that would be crueller. It might create an expec-

tation he could not fill. Better a small hurt now than
a large hurt later. If she was not just playing a game,
and he reluctantly suspected she was not, then
she deserved her dreams. Of love, of marriage. And
the part of him that was capable of loving a woman
was dead. It lay withered and frozen within
him.

'Rae said she's not going to be my mommy,' Billy
told him blithely.

He turned his attention to the boy, startled.
'What?'

'She said she's never going to be my mommy, but
that we could be friends instead. She might bake
some chocolate chip cookies, anyway. She said you
aren't her type.'

'Is that right?' Galen responded, his eyes seeking
out Rae's. He felt grateful, and oddly irked, too.
How the hell did she know if he was her type or not?
Not that he wanted to be. Not that he wasn't
thankful she wouldn't be plotting to capture him
while she was here. But he felt the smallest sense
of loss, too. A tiny, niggling doubt. That maybe he
had killed something before it had had a chance to
live.

That maybe it would have been nice to get to
know her—this mysterious woman with her
compelling eyes, who smelled of wild flowers and
made him think strange thoughts of hay and kisses.

He wondered if he had a fatal attraction for
women who were not good for him. Here she was.
Another city woman, completely foreign to the rural
life-style. Who, in two weeks, would miss being able
to call out for pizza, would miss the shops, the bright
lights, the amenities that a city offered and the
country did not. A woman, he reminded himself

sternly, callous enough, or silly enough, to shop for a marriage in a magazine.

'I'm going to invite Clarice for supper tomorrow,' he decided out loud.

Out of the corner of his eye he saw Billy make a face, but it was Rae he watched. Her face was carefully schooled, impassive. For some reason he felt disappointed at her lack of reaction.

'See you two at lunch,' he muttered, and made his way back down the ladder.

Rae watched Galen descend the ladder. She had held out that kitten like a flag of peace. His refusal had made her feel childish and stupid. But at least now she could dismiss him as a man as cold, as gloomy, as unfeeling as winter itself.

But she felt none of those things. In fact, she felt an unwanted stab of tenderness for the big man. For all that his features had been cold to the point of being disdainful, for a split second she had seen something else. When she had first seen him peering into the loft from his perch on the ladder, there had been an unspeakable agony in his eyes. It had disappeared in a flash, as soon as Billy had spotted him. But in that split second she had known that what Gramps had said was true. Galen was wounded—at least as scarred as she herself was. It made her sad. They were two essentially good people crippled by life—moving in the deadening state of the walking wounded.

'I wish Clarice wasn't coming for supper,' Billy said. 'She's awful.'

'Is she? Why?'

'Ah, she's always saying stuff like mind your manners, and children should be seen and not heard. She acts like she thinks she's my mother—

but not the nice kind like Jake has.'

'Billy, do you think she might be your mother some day?' She dreaded his answer. Because she liked him so much that she would want to help him accept the fact if she could—even though, for a reason she dared not contemplate, she did not want to help Billy accept another woman as Galen's wife. Not that she wanted the job herself. No, she most certainly did not. But she did want it to go to somebody whom Billy liked. Whom Gramps liked. Somebody tender and good who could help Galen with those hurts that were so naked in his eyes sometimes.

I am here to write an article, she reminded herself firmly. Not to get emotionally involved with this family. Not to try and solve any of their problems. Not to interfere. And yet she knew, after less than twenty-four hours, that she was already involved, because she cared. About this little boy. About Gramps. Yes, drat it all anyway, even about Galen. She had thought for a long time that you could turn off caring, quickly and efficiently, as though it were a light switch. She had thought that was the best way to protect oneself from the heartaches of life. But now she was forced to admit that it was part of her nature to care—and that not caring only created a hidden heartache of a different kind, a gaping emptiness, a life of winter without end.

'If my Dad ever marries Clarice, I'll run away from home,' Billy promised solemnly.

'That's not a very good idea, Billy,' she said sternly. 'How on earth would you look after yourself?'

'Gramps would look after me,' he said stoutly, ''cause he'd run away from home, too.'

'Wonderful,' she commented drily, her urge to interfere stronger than ever. She liked Gramps immensely, but he needed a darn good talking to.

She reminded herself again that it was not her position to interfere, and she turned her mind to the article. She needed some facts. Could Billy, at least in part, give them to her?

They strolled out of the barn towards the fields, Rae valiantly trying to ignore the fact that her feet were wet and uncomfortable, her trousers stained beyond repair.

'What kind of horse is Sugar?' she asked, beginning at a point where she thought he would be quite knowledgeable.

'A white one,' Billy informed her solemnly.

'But does she have a breed?'

'Nope.'

'And how about Bossy?'

'She's a milk cow,' Billy told her. 'And those ones are beef cattle.' He pointed at the herd over the fence.

Ah, now maybe they were getting somewhere.

'Do they have a breed?'

'Yup. They're Heffords.'

She couldn't very well ask him to spell that for her. She would have to look it up—somewhere. 'And do you have many of them?'

'I have one of my very own. A calf. For 4-H. Dad helped me pick him.'

'But how many does the farm have?'

'Lots,' Billy said helpfully.

She sighed, and accepted the fact that Billy was not going to be a source for more than a child's view of farm life—which was not part of her angle, as

delightful as it might have been. She had to admit a
bit of relief. She was not comfortable using Billy.
Not to get at Galen. And not even to ferret out a few
facts about the farm. She could not betray his trust
in her, even if he did not know she was doing it. She
would know.

'What's 4-H?' she asked him, but not for the
article.

'It stands for heads, hearts, hands . . .'

They finally finished their rather extensive tour of
the farm. The only other fact she had gleaned,
without probing, had been that much of Galen's
land lay on the other side of the creek. She planned
to put a few well-thought-out questions to him at
lunch, and went over in her mind how to word them
casually. Her interest should seem natural enough,
given her supposed intention to marry a farmer.
And, if Galen wouldn't answer her questions,
perhaps Gramps would. Again, she felt an
unwanted stab of guilt. Intellectually she could
rationalise what she was doing. But in her heart it
felt so dreadfully wrong to be here under false
pretences. To be using these people.

But what else could she do? Her job was her
lifeline. And they would never know what she
had done. A household full of men was unlikely to
have ever even heard of *Womanworld*, let alone ever
come across a copy of it. Besides, she wasn't even
using the mail-order-bride angle any more. There
was no chance of the family being recognised,
ridiculed. The piece could be set on any farm,
anywhere.

But, even as she talked to herself, she was
wondering something else. Did she want to make her
comeback with an article rooted in a deception?

Could she? Or would her reluctance, her own
doubts be there, between every line?

As she changed into her last clean outfit, she
debated just telling them the truth. That she was
really there to do an article on farm life, and would
they help her? But how would she deal with the
inevitable question of what had brought her here
originally? She would look like a liar and a conniver.
She was risking Gramps' and Billy's respect, not to
mention that she would no doubt confirm how Galen
felt about her anyway. She did not want to see
herself in that light, so she did not want to allow
others to see her in that light either. Especially not
Galen, she realised, coming face to face with the fact
that she wanted him to like her, or at least respect
her. And she knew he wouldn't if he knew the truth.
She did not feel strong enough to deal with a
deepening of his contempt. It would make being
stranded here for two weeks in his company
unbearable.

She sat on the bed, pondering. What if she had a
rough draft of the article ready before she left? What
if she came clean as she was on her way out of the
door? Could leave them with the evidence that she
was in no way going to hurt them? In fact, though
she had never before done this, she could give them
the final say on whether or not she could use the
article.

She felt a sense of relief. Yes, that was the route
she would go. And if they refused their permission
for her to use the article?

They wouldn't, she decided firmly. It was going
to be too good. And if, despite her best effort, they
did not want their way of life exposed to the public
eye—well, then she would have to accept that. She

was not going to rebuild her career on a betrayal. Because success would be meaningless if she had bought it at the price of her integrity.

There was another benefit to not telling them now what she was doing. They would be more natural, lacking in self-consciousness. She would see their life-style as it really was. She was well aware of how awkward people could become when they knew they were going to be the subject of a story.

'How did you like the farm?' Gramps asked when she came down for lunch.

She noted Galen did not even glance up from behind the pages of his newspaper when she entered the room.

'It's beautiful,' she answered sincerely.

Something that sounded like a snort came from behind the paper.

She glared at him. 'Well, isn't it?'

He lowered the paper and gave her his full attention. 'Farming isn't poetic. It goes a little deeper than pretty pictures of red barns on Christmas cards.'

'Thank you for enlightening me,' she said sarcastically, aware that Billy and Gramps were watching the scene with interest. 'Why don't you tell me what it is about?'

'It's about hard work. It's about dirt and sweat. It's about sixteen-hour days sometimes. It's about having baby chicks under a heat lamp in the kitchen, and maybe a lamb or two behind the stove. It's about being up to your elbows in muck and blood at three in the morning. It's about being up to your knees in cow manure. It's about having a face as black as a coal miner's after a day on the tractor underneath a blistering sun. Not very romantic stuff, Ms Douglas.'

'And you wouldn't trade it for the world,' she guessed softly.

'No, I wouldn't,' he agreed. 'But I was born to this way of life. I like the hard work, the earth, the elements. I like the realities of farming—not some sugar-coated version I have in my head.'

'But don't the realities include the beauty?' she asked stubbornly. 'Or are you indifferent to the freshness of the air, the endlessness of the sky, the curly coat of a newborn calf, the landscape, the solitude, the silence?'

His hard gaze had softened somewhat. 'No,' he admitted, 'I'm not indifferent to any of those things. But they're not the whole picture. And it would be dangerous for you to see a farm too romantically.'

'Well, I don't,' she sputtered.

'Don't you?' His tone was smooth, relentless. 'Then why don't you tell me everything you know about farms?'

'I don't know very much,' she admitted, but without apology, her chin lifted at the challenge in his eyes.

'Then why have you decided to marry a farmer?' he asked crisply. 'It seems to me like a hell of a funny reason to get married, because a man's a farmer. Or a doctor or a lawyer, for that matter. Are you intent on marrying a role, rather than a man? Don't you believe in love, for God's sake?'

'No, I don't,' she said coldly. 'Do you?'

For a second the barrier in his eyes came down, and she glimpsed his sadness.

'No, I guess I don't,' he admitted. 'I did once.'

'So did I,' she responded softly. 'That was enough.' For a moment their eyes locked and held, and she felt a bond of sympathy form between them.

He sensed it too, she suspected, because he snapped it before it had time to grow. 'Why does everybody want to get married if they don't believe in love?'

She answered thoughtfully, and from her heart. 'It's still possible to believe in other things, and other kinds of love. Like the love of a family —as you and Billy have. We all need something, Galen.'

'I still don't understand choosing a farmer,' he said, but she knew he had taken her point well.

'OK, I do have some romantic notions about the country. I won't apologise for them. I think it provides a healthy wholesome environment in which to raise children.' Thought she had never spent any time in the country, after her morning with Billy she was able to make that statement with absolute sincerity.

The most reluctant of affections passed through her eyes and then was gone. 'You still have no idea what the realities are,' he said gruffly, but not harshly.

'So show me,' she challenged him.

'I just might do that,' he said, his eyes lingering on her face, faintly troubled, faintly curious—as if he wanted to know her, and did not like the fact. Abruptly he looked away. 'Gramps, I'm inviting Clarice for dinner tomorrow night.'

'Well, don't expect me to cook. I don't like hearing unwanted tips on how to make my meals more interesting and nutritious.

But Rae wasn't listening. She was pondering that heady moment when she had seen something very like affection in Galen's eyes when he had looked at her. She was pondering the possibility that Clarice was being held up like a shield against her.

No, that wasn't possible. It was her imagination. Galen had made it quite clear how he felt about her. Or had he made it quite clear how he was trying to feel about her?

And why should she care? If anything, she should be disturbed by traces of curiosity, a hint of reluctant liking coming from Galen. It would only complicate her situation unbearably. Because she was not really a woman looking for a husband. Because she was no longer interested in love.

So why was her heart beating a painful tatoo within her chest, and why, when she saw him looking at her again, a thoughtful frown creasing his rocky features, did a blush that she suspected would put the dawn to shame creep like fire up her cheeks?

CHAPTER SIX

THE next morning Galen made Billy call his teacher and get assignments so that he would not fall behind on his school work. After breakfast, and after trying every argument possible, Billy reluctantly retreated to the den with his school books.

'Could I come?' Rae asked Galen as he headed for the door.

'No.' Without offering elaboration, excuses, or explanations he was gone.

Rae stared after him, furious. By now, she thought, she should have accepted the fact the man was cold and rude and quite insufferable. By now she should have hardened herself to the fact that he was going to ignore her completely, as he had last night, or treat her a bit like a bothersome fly, as he had every time she had attempted to draw him out in conversation.

Of course, by now, she should have also become immune to his attractions. It should be something like buying a fine painting. At first you enjoyed it immensely, and looked at it at every opportunity, but finally it was just 'there', so much a part of your surroundings that you barely ever noticed it.

But every time she looked at Galen she noticed something new about him. The deep crinkles at the sides of his eyes, the faintly sardonic quirk at the corner of his mouth, his habit of pushing his heavy hair back off his forehead, how his eyes darkened

and lightened, giving away things that that
impassive face never would.

It's only been a little more than a day, she told
herself. She would get used to being at such close
quarters with such an aggravatingly attractive man.
By this time next week, she wouldn't even notice
how those broad shoulders strained within the faded
fabric of his workshirt, how his faded jeans moulded
to the powerful muscle of his legs. By this time next
week, she would be completely indifferent to the fact
that he did everything—from reaching for a salt
shaker to unfolding his long length from a
chair—with an innate and magnificent grace. Yes,
by this time next week she would have succeeded in
delegating that powerful presence to the woodwork.
She would be able to see him simply professionally,
as a man who had some facts that she wanted.
Period.

Liar, a little voice within taunted her. OK, she
responded waspishly to the voice, but given time, a
year, or maybe two, everything about him would
just be one giant bore.

Liar, the voice repeated cheerfully. And she had
to admit she knew it was a lie. He was too complex
ever to be boring. There were too many dimensions,
there was too much fire lurking beneath those cold
features, but flickering away in those incredible
black eyes. Given a lifetime to know him, then
maybe. No, probably not even then.

Gramps chuckled behind her, and, forcing her
features into an expression of cool uncaring, she
turned and looked at him.

'Man's running scared,' he noted fiendishly.

'Oh, bosh!' she said sharply. 'That man hasn't
known a moment's fear in his entire life.'

'He's just a man, Rae. And we all know fear, no matter how good we get at hiding it. Wouldn't have hurt him to let you tag along. Wouldn't have hurt him a bit, if he didn't give two hoots about you. Interesting that he wouldn't let you go, wouldn't you say?'

'I would not say that at all,' Rae said firmly, but something leapt within her. She forced herself not to dwell on Gramps' foolishness. 'Would you mind if I made Billy some cookies to take the sting out of his having to do his schoolwork?'

'Fine idea.'

She busied herself mixing batter, casually grilling Gramps as she moved about the kitchen. 'Heffords' proved to be Herefords, 'lots' proved to be two hundred head. The farm comprised two sections of land, and the MacNamaras mix-farmed. Some livestock, some crops. It was exactly the kind of information she needed, she told herself. But she felt guilty about getting it. And even worse, the facts weren't filling the hole she wanted filled. What she wanted to know about was sweat and dirt. What was really involved in making it all work. She wanted to be there at Galen's side, for purely professional reasons only, of course, so she could get a feel for it all.

Liar, that aggravating little voice said again.

Oh, hell, she thought fiercely, it's true. I want to breathe the same air he breathes, see his world through his eyes, see the sweat beading on the satin of his skin, smell his scent. But only because I'm a writer. Only because that's how I have to experience things to make them come alive for others.

Only because he's the most intriguing human being I've ever come in contact with, and I want to know him. Inside and outside, and as much as one person could ever know another.

And that, she knew, was something more than a professional interest. And she knew she had better kill it quickly—rather than risk it killing her.

The morning passed swiftly, and it was fun. Gramps was a wonderfully entertaining companion, and of course Billy crept down the stairs once or twice to snatch cookies and to find out what was going on.

Galen reappeared at lunch time, dirty and sweaty. Though he cleaned up at the sink in the back porch before coming in to the kitchen, she discovered she was not repulsed by these things, as he had insinuated she would be, and as she had known she would not be. No, there was something almost unbearably attractive about a man who did hard work, who was not ashamed to mingle with the earth, to feel a cooling sweat break out over his body.

'Clarice is coming for supper?' Gramps asked.

'Yes. I ran over there this morning.'

'What are you cooking?'

Galen glared at him.

'Told you I ain't cookin' for her,' Gramps said stubbornly.'

'So don't,' Galen shot back. 'I'll cook.'

'Oh, Dad,' Billy said scornfully. 'All you can make is hamburger mash, and it's yucky.' He brightened. 'That's OK, though.'

Rae smiled secretively. Yes, it was OK to feed somebody you didn't like something 'yucky'.

'Course, I might be persuaded to cook,' Gramps said slyly.

Galen looked both relieved and suspicious.
'What's your price?'

'That you don't embarrass Rae.'

'What do you mean?'

'Well, Clarice is gonna have some questions
about Rae being here. I don't think she needs to
know the whole truth.'

Rae shot the old man a grateful look. She hadn't
even given a thought to how her presence was going
to be explained to Clarice. In fact, she had been
scrupulously avoiding thinking about Clarice
coming here at all.

'People shouldn't ever do things that are going to
make them ashamed,' Galen said quietly, his eyes
resting on Rae's face.

'I haven't done anything I'm ashamed of,' Rae
said bravely, though she hated the idea of Clarice
knowing how she had come to be here. It was going
to be very awkward. But pride forced her to push
on. 'You can tell your girlfriend whatever you
please.'

'She's not my girlfriend.'

Something very like surprise crossed Galen's
features, as if those were not the words he had
meant to speak. Billy grinned. Gramps winked at
Rae.

'Clarice is just a friend,' Galen said with gruff
defensiveness, scowling at Billy and Gramps.

'So what are you going to tell her about Rae?'
Gramps pressed.

Galen's eyes rested on Rae again. 'I wouldn't
have ever embarrassed you intentionally,' he told
her, his voice husky, unintentionally sensual.
'Gramps didn't need to buy that from me.'

She stared back at him, surprised, and oddly

thrilled, too. He had just admitted something. That
he didn't find her as objectionable as he had hoped
to find her. That some reluctant part of him cared
about her, and that he would not hurt her
feelings—intentionally. Or was she reading too
much into it? He was not the kind of man who hurt
people intentionally, regardless of how he felt about
them. Not like another man she had known. He was
not at all like that other man. Was that a part of
what made him so attractive to her? A very large
part? That he was Roger's complete opposite?

'We'll tell Clarice she's a friend of the family, and
leave it at that,' Galen said. 'Considering how you
and Billy have taken to our guest, I don't think
that's stretching the truth too much.'

She noticed he volunteered nothing about how he
felt. She knew that, at least, was completely
intentional. But she was unoffended by it. She
suspected, again with that funny little thrill in
the pit of her stomach, that Galen did not know how
he felt.

Any more than I myself do, she reminded herself.

She spent the afternoon in her room, writing. She
did not have a lot to write about yet, but she began
to put in the rough lines, adding splashes of colour
here and there, grouping together her facts. Writing
had always completely engrossed her, had always
provided her with a different world to escape into.
Even when she had been so completely taken with
Roger, he had never interfered with this, never
entered her sanctuary of mind. It was only after
she'd discovered the truth about him that her
mind had been in such a tumult it had affected her
work.

But this afternoon her concentration was shot to pieces. She felt disproportionately nervous about meeting Clarice. Her mind kept straying to Galen—as did her eyes. She could see him out of her window, tossing bales out of the barn loft with an unbelievable ease.

Poetry. Muscle being put to work by mind. His strength being pitted against an obstacle with such grace and ease that what he was doing appeared to be both effortless and enjoyable.

She wished he would move on to something else, where she did not have to look at him. Of course, not looking at him would have been as easy as lowering her blind, which she could not bring herself to do. She liked looking at him. God, she liked looking at him. She wished she had a camera. She wanted to capture him, this moment of harmony between a man and his body and a man and the earth. But she realised that a picture would not capture that elusive thing she was trying for. A picture would only stir in her the same longing she felt now. A longing without a name, or a reason. To be a part of that scene, a part of him, instead of a wistful observer.

She snapped the blind shut, her wandering thoughts frightening her. It didn't really help. She just kept lifting it back up to peep out and see if he was still there, if that strange magic in the air around him was still casting its spell over her. It was. Damn it all, anyway, it was.

She wished suddenly that she could go home. And was glad, oh, so glad, that she could not.

Clarice appeared promptly at six, pulling up to the house in a pick-up truck. Rae was dressed casually—what choice did she have?—in an outfit

that gave her an I-don't-give-a-damn look that she
had worked quite hard to accomplish. She wanted
her look to say she did not feel threatened, did not
feel like she was in competition with this woman.
She wasn't after all. So why did her jeans, her
uncurled hair, her crisp cotton shirt, feel like a
disguise?

Rae sat in the living-room, thumbing a magazine,
watching from behind the curtain of her lashes as the
woman left her truck. She jumped down from the
cab with an athletic grace, and Rae felt her heart fall
already. Clarice's movements were like
Galen's—smooth and confident. She didn't even
look ridiculous clomping along in her
gumboots—just as Galen did not look ridiculous in
his.

I would look ridiculous in gumboots, Rae thought
woefully. Why did she care? She didn't belong to
this world.

Clarice came to the front door—the company
door—Rae noted with small satisfaction. Very small
and very brief.

She did not know what she had expected, but it
had not been this. Clarice had platinum blonde hair,
green, slanting eyes, a wide, sensual mouth. She rid
herself of the gumboots, and slipped into a pair of
heels, adding to her height and her stature.

She's a farmer? Rae thought incredulously. She
should have been a model. Easily. Her dress was
very plain, a jade-green that matched her eyes, but
out of a hard-wearing, cheap fabric. But on Clarice
the dress would have looked quite at home on the
cover of *Vogue*.

Introductions were made, and Clarice regarded
Rae briefly with a narrowed, measuring gaze, and

then appeared to dismiss her. Just as she appeared to
dismiss both Gramps and Billy after the briefest of
greetings. Her focus went to Galen and stayed there
for the remainder of the evening. They talked
between themselves, about farming. Most of the
time it could have been Greek to Rae, though she
watched their interaction with carefully concealed
interest, and a falling heart.

They were cut from the same mould, Galen and
Clarice. It went further than the fact they were both
so physically pleasing to the eye. They were both
strong. Extremely confident. Informed. Committed
to their way of life.

But Rae couldn't help noticing that the qualities
that made Galen so attractive did not do that for
Clarice. Her no-nonsense practicality was not
tempered with even a hint of gentleness. Her
strength was a hard-bitten variety, and her
confidence was such that it tolerated no one else's
views or opinions. She had little patience with Billy,
and even less with Gramps.

I'd run away, too, Rae found herself thinking.
The woman had the heart of a marine drill
instructor. It was obvious to Rae, through the other
woman's efficiency of movement, and her concise
conversation, that Clarice lived in a well-ordered
world of her own making, and she would try to force
anyone she ever lived with into her moulds. She
would live by a rigid rule book that would be
intolerable to two irrepressible renegades like Billy
and Gramps.

And Galen? Well, Galen was strong enough to
hold his own against this woman. Strong enough
that he probably didn't even realise how
overpowering she was.

He treated her with friendly affection, and respect. Good God, he even teased her now and then. More than once he touched her, his hand covering hers, stroking her shoulder for a moment, when he got up to pour coffee. And he was as locked in to her as she was to him. It was as if nobody else was at the dinner-table with them.

Rae felt her head beginning to pound ruthlessly, as supper dragged on. Clarice's presence was forcing her to acknowledge that her own feelings for Galen were ridiculously strong, given the short length of time she had known him. Ridiculously strong, and ridiculously hopeless.

Finally, to her relief, Clarice announced she had to go as she would be up very early in the morning.

Galen saw her to the door, kissed her lightly on the cheek. Rae wanted to bolt from the room to hide how that kiss twisted at her heart.

'I'm going to bed,' she announced quietly, before Galen returned.

'Wait just a second,' Gramps said mischievously, pouring her another cup of coffee.

Galen came and sat back down, and Gramps poured him another cup of coffee, too.

'Quite a show, son,' he said casually, when he was once again seated.

'Pardon?' Galen said coldly.

'Well, it's just that I ain't never seen you quite so lovey-dovey with Clarice, that's all.'

'Lovey-dovey?' Galen growled incredulously, but a column of red was moving up his throat and suffusing his face.

'Yeah, Dad. You don't ever kiss Clarice goodbye. Yuk!'

'You stay out of this,' Galen commanded

furiously, and Billy sat back with startled surprise.

'Now, don't get excited, Galen,' Gramps said calmly. 'I just wondered about it, is all.'

'There's nothing to wonder about,' Galen said, biting out each word with careful control. 'I did not act any differently with Clarice than I ever do.' But his face was ruddy with either anger or embarrassment, and he would not look at Rae.

'Well, that's just fine, son,' Gramps said soothingly. 'Just thought I noticed something. That's all. Just thought a man who acts in an unusual way is usually trying to hide something about what he's really feeling. Guess I was mistaken. I apologise.'

'You're damned right you were mistaken!' Galen shot at him furiously. He glared at Rae, too, as if she was part of this conspiracy to unveil him. 'I happen to think very highly of Clarice.' He hesitated only a moment, and then the force of his fury seemed to carry him. 'I happen to be thinking of marrying her!'

'That a fact?' Gramps said, unperturbed. 'You sound a bit like a man running scared to me, Galen MacNamara.'

Rae watched Galen wide-eyed, feeling Gramps was really pushing too far. The muscles in Galen's jaw were working with a leashed anger that was quite frightening. She noticed his mighty fist was clenching and unclenching, and was surprised by her calm knowledge that Gramps was in no danger from the storm that brewed in those awesome eyes.

'Running scared of what?' Galen asked with dangerous quiet.

Gramps shrugged. 'You tell me.'

And then Rae was aware that every eye at the table had automatically turned to her, including Galen's. His eyes were shooting white-hot sparks, and her cheeks ignited with heat.

But the defensive denial in his coal-black gaze faded, and a thoughtful, puzzled frown creased his forehead as he studied her. She suspected he was also being man enough to study himself—and didn't like what he was coming up with.

The tension of trying to figure out what thoughts had brought that unfathomable look to his eyes was unbearable. Rae practically leapt up from the table.

'Excuse me,' she stammered, and then turned on her heel and fled.

The tension did not ease in the next few days. Galen ignored her almost totally. She returned the treatment studiously. And yet, Rae was only too aware that it was on the surface. Beneath the surface, their awareness of each other was almost electrical.

She knew the moment he walked into a room, because the hair on the back of her neck would prickle as if she was being watched. She was aware that she knew the sound of his step, and that her heart strained to hear it. She was aware that she knew the rich, male scent of him, and that she drank it in with a craving that could not be satisfied. She was aware that the ways he moved and spoke were being burned on to her brain, and at night she was kept awake contemplating some small gesture he had made, the texture of his voice, the moods that deepened his eyes.

And she was also aware that he was not as indifferent to her as he struggled to appear. That awareness, too, was in little things. Insignificant things. Once, when she was helping with the dishes, he reached to the cupboard over her head to get a coffee-mug down. His hand rested briefly on her shoulder, in a gesture so completely natural that for a moment he didn't even notice. And then he yanked his hand back and stared at it accusingly, as though it had betrayed him. At night, when she played with Billy, she was aware of his gaze resting on her with disturbing intensity, until he realised he was staring, and then he would quickly leave the room or go back to what he had been doing. If she inadvertently touched him while passing him a plate at dinner, he would recoil from her touch, and then scowl in recognition that he had over-reacted. He disappeared for hours on end, returning to the house with the reluctance of a man who was trying to outrun something he could not outrun.

Because it was there. A sizzle in the air when their eyes met. A hunger in their gazes.

It's just because we're two normal, healthy adults caught in the most awkward of circumstances, Rae would tell herself. Isn't it natural that we would both start to feel a certain base attraction—rooted in the close proximity we're forced to live in? She hoped acknowledging her feelings would make them go away. But it didn't.

It was still there, growing stronger, and she recognised that they both over-compensated in their efforts to deny its growing power over them. He snapped at her when he had to speak to her. She snapped back. He mentioned Clarice at every opportunity. She talked about the mystery farmer she intended to marry.

'Yup. Running scared.' Gramps declared with satisfaction when Galen did not appear for lunch for the third day in a row.

'Oh, shut up!' Rae finally commanded, having heard that particular phrase just once too often.

Gramps, unoffended, raised a bushy eyebrow at her. Grinned. 'Make that two running scared,' he declared with utter and aggravating satisfaction.

She tried desperately to lose herself in her writing. It was a strategy that had worked when she'd had a crush on Bill Carruthers in university. It had always filled the hours quite satisfactorily when Roger had broken a date—again. So she forced herself to spend every afternoon working on her article. But putting pen to paper did not have the magic she had always relied on it to have. Nothing came. From that wonderful imagination that she had thought would always be there to fill in the gaps in her life, she drew a big zero. She could force words on to paper, but she could not force them to live, to breathe, to dance. She wrote the same dry and dull drivel that had placed her career at *Womanworld* in such a precarious position.

Hearts, she thought angrily, as she penned a few postcard-pretty phrases that did not capture that which she wanted to capture. They interfered when they were broken and now it appeared they interfered even worse when they were on the mend.

She sighed. She had not wanted to admit that. That her heart was on the mend. No. Healed. Ready to be hurt again.

She forced herself to read through what she had just written. It was so empty. The essential was missing. The essence of farm life. The spirit of it. Galen.

She needed Galen to do what she wanted to do. She needed to know about dirt and sweat. She needed to feel the dirt on her hands and the sweat running down her back. She knew the time had come to beard the lion in his den.

For the sake of the article.

No, she admitted with disgust, throwing down her pencil and crumpling a piece of paper that held too many purple phrases about birds chirping and cattle lowing. For the sake of her soul.

From nowhere, tears sprang up, welled in her eyes, slithered silently down her cheeks. She knew then that Gramps had spoken the truth. She was running scared. From love. And she knew, her relief mixed with terror, that she was running out of places to run. That they were both running out of places to run.

CHAPTER SEVEN

'GALEN,' Rae announced the next night at dinner, 'I'm bored.' For the first time in days she felt she had his full attention.

'I guess that doesn't surprise me very much,' he said, giving her a look that came very close to being sympathetic. 'City people just don't know what's involved in a rural life-style, Rae. I'm glad you found out before you had too much invested in it.'

She suspected he was also congratulating himself for investing nothing in getting to know her, since she had now lived up to his expectations. Or so he thought.

'Oh,' she said sweetly, 'you misunderstood me. I'm not bored with farm life. I don't even feel as if I've had a chance to taste it. I'm bored because I've run out of things to do. I've walked every inch of this farm. I've read all your magazines. I've got enough chocolate chip cookies in your freezer to last you into next year.'

His expression had become wary now.

'I don't see that there's anything I can do about that,' he said uncooperatively.

'Oh, but there is, Galen! You told me I had the wrong idea about farms. And I can see now that you were absolutely right. There's obviously more to it than breathing in the wonderful air, and playing with the kittens. Show me!' Those last two words came out with far more plea than she had intended.

'I don't owe you anything,' he said, but the words were oddly without sting. 'Look, I'm not responsible for your being here, and I'm not responsible for the fact that you're bored.'

'No, you're not,' she agreed reasonably. 'But what would it hurt for you to let me tag along with you for a day? Just one day, Galen. And then maybe I would find out that I didn't like it, wasn't cut out for it. Wouldn't it be better for me to find out now, rather than after I'm married——'

'You know, Rae, just as I'm starting to think you're a fairly sensible woman, you bring that up again. I don't know who you are. Most of the time you don't strike me as being a flake.'

Most of the time? she thought. But at least she knew he was noticing her more than he ever let on. She even sensed that he, very reluctantly, was growing to like her and respect her.

'Maybe one day is all it would take to make me change my mind about that, too, Galen. Maybe you're right. I shouldn't marry a farmer. But how would I know?'

'Oh, you'll know,' he said. 'I think you're right. I think one day is all it should take. Be here, in the kitchen, at five tomorrow morning.'

'I will be,' she said eagerly. 'Thank you, Galen.'

'By this time tomrrow you'll know you don't have a thing to thank me for,' he snapped, and then added with satisfaction, 'Yes, by this time tomorrow I think your romantic notions about farming should be firmly laid to rest, Ms Douglas. You'll probably try to swim out of here to get back to your advertising job.'

She felt a niggle of doubt bite into her sense
of victory. What exactly had she let herself in
for?

Rae surveyed herself in the mirror early the next
morning. Well, she certainly looked ready for
work—if the job intended was keeping birds out of
the crops. She could have easily put two of her in the
huge man's shirt that Gramps had provided her
with. And two of her into the jeans that were cinched
at the waist and rolled at the cuff. She plopped the
cap with the 'Runs Like a Deer' caption on her
head, and was aghast. She looked about as feminine
and sexy as Billy looked. Somehow she didn't think
Clarice dressed like this to go about her day.

Rae looked longingly at her other choices, and
knew them to be entirely unsutable. She had already
practically destroyed one outfit from her meagre
wardrobe, she could hardly sacrifice another one.
Besides, she wanted Galen to see she was serious
about this. She wanted him to see she wasn't
completely oblivious to the realities. Which is
certainly what he would have to think if she made
her appearance in her Angora sweater.

She could already hear him in the kitchen, and she
quickly turned from the unsatisfying reflection in the
mirror and went down to join him.

He turned from the coffeemaker when she came
in, surveyed her solemnly, and then turned back to
his task—through not before she had seen the
glimmer of amusement dash through his eyes and
tug at his stern lips.

Damn him to death, she thought waspishly, for
looking so magnificently attractive without half

trying. He was dressed in a workshirt in the ugliest shade of green she had ever seen. His jeans were so old and faded that one false move would disintegrate them. But he didn't look like a scarecrow. No, he looked compellingly strong, hard, lean.

'What can I do?' she asked, hoping she sounded more chipper than she felt.

'Well, since you ask,' he said smoothly, 'you can split some kindling and get the fire going in the stove.'

She glared at his broad back, and then at the pot-bellied black stove in the corner. She had always thought those things were decorations, until she had seen the MacNamaras actually using theirs. She had avoided the thing since arriving. It looked dangerous. In the life she led, if you wanted heat, you waltzed across the room and turned up the thermostat.

She reminded herself that was exactly the point. To find out, in intimate detail, about a life she didn't lead.

Galen had turned and raised an eyebrow at her hesitation. 'Axe is on the porch,' he said softly.

And a touch smugly, she thought, and stomped out on to the porch. She had a tough time making kindling. It was harder than it had looked when she had watched Gramps do it. By the time she had a tiny handful, she had broken into a sweat.

There, she thought with satisfaction. I have ingredient number one. Sweat. She brought in her small offering to Galen.

'Stove's over there,' he said easily, sipping on his coffee.

She was all too aware of his dark gaze resting on her when she opened the door of the stove to stuff in the small pieces of wood. A black cloud exited and nearly suffocated her.

'You might have warned me,' she said hotly when she heard the rumble of laughter behind her.

'For one, I didn't think it would be going from last night, and two, I thought you'd know enough to open the damper.'

'What the hell is a damper?' she muttered.

'You might want to bring in a few armloads of wood,' Galen suggested.

She had asked, she thought as she stomped back out to the porch, to learn a little about farm life. She had not thought she was signing on as slave for the day. The despicable cad was still sipping coffee as she marched back and forth with her arms aching and full of wood. She could feel splinters clinging to her. She suspected she had soot on her face.

She wondered if she should just quit now. After all, she did have both ingredients: sweat and dirt. But she knew she wouldn't give him the satisfaction. Besides, it wasn't that bad. In fact, it felt not bad at all to be giving long unused muscles a bit of a workout. And she supposed a farm wife would have to know how to use the stove.

Finally, when she had brought in enough wood to last three days, she helped herself to a coffee and sank into a chair across from Galen. She had taken exactly two sips when he glanced at his watch.

'Time to do the milking,' he said, getting to his feet.

'Could I finish my coffee?'

'The thing about having a milk cow is that you have to milk at the same time every day.'

'And that time is now,' she guessed drily.

'If you can't handle it, just say so,' he challenged, a wicked grin licking at his lips.

She met his gaze stubbornly, well aware he was going to try and break her. 'I can handle anything you throw at me, and then some,' she said leaping to her feet. 'Lead on.'

He made her go up in the loft and pitch down a bale for Bossy to munch while they milked.

'Are you going to do anything today?' she called. 'I wanted to see what a farm wife did. I don't necessarily have to have hands-on experience at everything.' She resisted the impulse to knead her already aching back.

He shrugged. 'You have to be strong for this way of life. It's very physical. Most of the families I know, everybody pitches in and does the chores. One day him, one day her, one day the kids. If you're not strong enough, you might as well find out now.' He looked thoughtful. 'I'm not trying to wear you down. I never gave it a thought. Clarice does all her chores.'

That settled it, Rae thought stubbornly. He could ask her to lift a two-ton wieght, and she'd figure out some way to do it. If Clarice could do this kind of stuff, day in and day out—well, then, so could she.

She was coming down out of the loft when the toe of her shoe caught in one of the ladder rungs, and she felt herself twist and start to fall. But the fall never happened. Two strong arms grabbed her from mid-air, and she felt herself being set firmly on the ground, though he did not let go of her.

For a moment she stood with her nose pressed into the rock-hard surface of his chest, feeling a strange contentment seep through her. As if this was where she belonged, in this man's arms, enveloped by his strength and his scent. Reluctantly she pulled away, but his hands did not unlock their hold on the small of her back.

'Thank you,' she stammered.

Still he did not let go, his dark eyes fastened on her own. Her eyes widened and her mouth parted faintly under the curious intensity of his gaze. He's going to kiss me, she thought, and a wave of pleasure crept through her, warming her and making her feel oddly drugged.

Instead he let go of her abruptly, and she backed up a step from him, mortified. What on earth had she been thinking of? What had he been thinking of? Good God, what if he had guessed how she was anticipating that kiss? What if even now he could sense the heavy beat of her heart, see the quickening of her breath, made visible by the frosty morning air?

And, even though she was mortified by her reaction, she could not let it go.

'I think I was very nearly kissed,' she was shocked to hear herself say. She was even more shocked by her provocative tone. No, this could not be reserved, shy, awkward-around-men Rae Douglas who was leaning towards this man invitingly.

She had never felt an urge this strong before, a curiosity so intense. She wanted to know what it would be like to be kissed by this man—would die to know. Roger had never made her feel like this.

Wanton. Devil-may-care. He had never inspired in
her this overwhelming thirst to know him in every
way a woman could know a man—spiritually,
physically, emotionally. Roger had been a romance. But a friend? A partner? A soulmate? A
lover?

She realised the potential had never existed
between she and Roger for a relationship as multi-
faceted as a diamond, as deep as the sea, as endless as the universe. But now she sensed, with some
deep inner intuition, as old, as reliable as the
earth, that that potential existed right here, right
now.

Galen, with a sharp intake of breath, took a step
towards her, his dark, sparkling eyes telling her that
he felt it, too. A command from destiny. To know
her. Explore her. Discover her. The very air
between them seemed to crackle with electrical
promise. Once again her heart leapt at the prospect
of those hard lips and arms claiming her, of those
eyes branding her for all time . . . but then the
moment died with the disappointing fizzle of a wet
firecracker.

His eyes became remote, his tone restrained.
'What happened is that you very nearly broke your
neck.' He turned from her swiftly. 'Bossy is getting
impatient.'

She wanted to turn and run. He had been right.
Only it had not even taken the whole day, and
already she was prepared to swim the creek to get
away from him. But she tilted her nose up proudly,
schooled her features into uncaring. She had an
article to write, and dammit, she could be
professional about getting her information. She
didn't even feel guilty about her deception in this

moment. She was glad she was doing it, and s
hoped it would hurt him when he found out. S
hoped it would twist like a knife in that ha
heart—just as his rejection of her twisted
hers.

She watched coldly as Galen demonstrated how
milk a cow. It looked easy enough. But then s
tried it. It was far more difficult than it looked
coax milk from a cow.

'This isn't much like what they show in t
movies,' she muttered with frustration.

'Not much of life is like what they show in t
movies,' Galen answered softly, and she turned a
looked at him. There was a sadness in his voi
even a trace of apology. As if he was trying to tell h
he was too disillusioned a man to believe in t
places that an exploratory kiss would have be
destined to take them.

Somehow his statement eased the tension betwe
them, and when he offered to finish the milking s
let him, and gladly. Her hands were cramped fr
the effort, she severely doubted she would ev
stand up straight again, and there were only a f
drops of milk in the bucket to show for all her
forts.

'It just takes practice. You can try aga
tomorrow.'

Oh, hurrah. 'Let's just take dairy farmers off
list.'

'Actually, a dairy farmer milks by machine th
days.'

'There's a machine that does this?' she ask
accusingly.

'There is, but I don't have one. It's hardly wo
it because when we're just milking for our perso

requirements. Besides, I kind of like doing some things the old and slow way.' Unfortunately, nostalgia is not a luxury you can afford in most aspects of farming these days. But I like morning chores. I never ask Billy or Gramps to do them. It's my time. Something like a meditation. The new day is so quiet, simple, tranquil.' He clammed up suddenly, as if he was uneasy about revealing too much of himself. But he already had, and she was entranced by this other and deeper side to Galen.

He put a piece of clean cheesecloth over the milk bucket and placed it on the floor in the cab of the truck.

Morning had broken now, dawn sending pink fingers of light washing over the entire farm. It was beautiful—like a painting frozen in time. He was right. There was an irresistible peace and tranquillity in this. It further eased the tension that had existed between them earlier, and now the silence between them had become comfortable and companionable as he passed her a large wicker basket and they headed to the henhouse.

There weren't very many chickens—again, Galen explained, he kept them only to satisfy their personal requirements.

'It's probably cheaper to buy eggs,' he admitted wryly, 'but it gives me a good feeling to be almost entirely self-sufficient. I wonder if it's the pioneer spirit in a man that makes him so proud to rely only on himself?'

For everything, she thought silently. And as much as she respected his self-sufficiency, she wondered if he had not taken it a step too far. His fierce independence seemed to extend to his emotional life, and that probably wasn't good. But then again, she didn't know the status of his relationship with Clarice, though she was beginning to suspect it wasn't nearly as red-hot as Gramps and Billy believed it to be. Galen simply didn't give off the signals of a man seriously involved else- where—or was that just wishful thinking on her part?

She sighed. The more she got to know this man, the more compelling she found him. She had better watch herself, or her poor bruised heart would be taking another beating when the bridge was re- placed and she left this place—and this man— forever.

Rae loathed the chickens immediately. The smelled terrible, they were blank-eyed, ugly and bad-tempered.

'Let's take chicken farmers off the list, too,' she suggested as she peered into the nests looking for eggs.

Galen laughed. 'I know it's pretty difficult to feel any affection for a chicken. On the other hand, wait until you taste these eggs—with half the cholesterol and twice the protein of a supermarket egg.'

'Really?' Rae asked over her shoulder, trying desperately not to show how his laughter had gone like a shiver of sunshine down her spine. 'How do I get Henrietta Hen out of this nest so I can see if there are any eggs under her?'

'Just slide your hand under.'

'She'll bite me,' Rae protested.

Galen came over and slipped his hand under the bird. She blinked with stupid placidness, and he brought out an egg.

'I left one under there for you.'

'You're all heart.' Rae imitated his gesture, and Henrietta Hen promptly pecked her.

Rae jumped back from her attacker, and then laughed. 'OK, I don't blame you. I guess it's not too hard to figure out I don't like you—and why should you give your eggs to someone who doesn't like you, hmm?'

Galen noticed the little peck was bleeding. Rae promptly stuck the injured finger in her mouth. No tears. No hysteria. No raging about the possibility of blood disease. He felt an incredible desire to start again where they had left off at the bottom of the ladder. And he knew he would fight that desire by trying harder than ever to make her quit—make her understand she just wasn't up to the hard manual labour involved in farming. This was no farm woman, and the sooner they both accepted that, the better.

Rae didn't know how hard he was trying, but she did know she had never worked quite so hard in her entire life. She fed cattle. She hauled water. She moved bales. She helped dig some new postholes, and repair a sagging fence.

The restraint between them slowly dissipated. They sparred with one another, but talked and laughed, too. There was something about shared exertion that made friendship—or at least companionship—come easily and naturally.

'Well, what do you think about farm life now?' Galen asked as they drove back towards the house, the sun sinking in the western sky.

Rae was so tired that her head was lolling against her chest. But she gave him a weary smile.

'I think it's wonderful.'

He shot her a disbelieving look, saw that she was looking thoughtfully and appreciatively out of the window at the setting sun.

'I mean, it's exhausting. I don't know when I've felt so tired. But, Galen, it was exhilarating, too! Working so hard. Being outside. Feeling like a part of the environment. Seeing the result of what you're doing, right now. The day went by so fast. It's crazy. I ache as I've never ached. And yet I feel so good. I feel strong. I feel as if I've really accomplished something with this day.' She did not add that she had felt like this sometimes when she was writing—so involved, so absorbed in the moment that the day flew by, leaving her pleasantly exhausted, and yet feeling wonderfully contented and self-satisfied.

She turned and caught him staring at her. She grinned wearily, and closed her eyes. 'It doesn't matter whether you believe me.'

But he believed her. He studied the line of her relaxed face. Remembered how hard she had worked. She'd been a real trooper, refusing nothing, giving everything her best shot. Trying everything with such enthusiasm, even when her energy was dying near the end of the day. He knew there had been something about her he could not put his finger on. Had not wanted to put his finger on. She'd been happy. The glow in her face had just been growing all day long. And he didn't think it had that much to do with the sunshine.

She's going to make some farmer a damn fine wife, he found himself thinking, making himself tear his eyes away from the appeal of her sun-kissed face. For a reason he wasn't at all prepared to investigate, the idea did not thrill him at all.

CHAPTER EIGHT

RAE appeared in the kitchen early the following morning. The only change in her appearance from the previous day was that she was wearing a red plaid shirt instead of a blue one.

Galen looked up at her with surprise. From the warmth in the kitchen, she could tell the stove was already going. He hadn't expected her. For some reason that disappointed her.

'I hoped maybe I could come with you again,' she said in a low voice, feeling shy and vulnerable. They seemed to have made such headway yesterday. There were times when things had been so easy and fun between them. But if he said no, they would be back at square one.

She dared not think, square one of what, exactly? In all honesty she had all the information she needed for her article. And in all honesty she knew she should not encourage a relationship with Galen. She could not survive being hurt again. Not so soon. And she was not at all sure that that was not where all relationships ended—with a brutal and lasting hurt.

And yet she could not fight this thing within her, either. This yearning to be with him. To feel the sunshine of his laughter, to bask in the shadow of his strength. Being with him did something to her—made her feel electrically alive, made her feel as if the world had gone from black to white to full colour. She greedily wanted more of what she had felt yesterday. And today she could not bring herself to worry about the price she might pay tomorrow.

She was uncomfortably aware, from his silence, that he wrestled with the decision whether to allow her to come. Her heart fell with the despairing thought that he had not enjoyed her company as much as she had enjoyed his—then rocketed upwards as she wondered if perhaps he had enjoyed it must as much, and, like her, was trying to outdistance a future hurt.

The silence lengthened, and suddenly she could no longer bear his eyes resting on her with such turmoil.

She turned, crestfallen, hoping it didn't show. 'I'm sorry,' she murmured. 'You told me morning was your time, and I shouldn't have intruded.'

'No!' The word exploded behind her. She turned and saw he looked faintly embarrassed by his vehemence. 'You can come. I'm just surprised you want to—especially since you seemed to be up rather late last night.'

Her heart did another rollercoaster ride—soaring at the way some part of him had won out over his iron will, and then plummeting at his inadvertent reminder of her treachery.

She looked at him warily. Had there been suspicion in the way he had noted she'd been up late? Of course not. He couldn't possibly know that she had been labouring over her article, bone-tired and yet so eager to get it down.

She grinned at him. 'Thank you,' she said softly.

*   *   *

After that she just got up every morning and went with him. In the days that followed she mucked out the barn, moved grain, helped a cow give birth. It was dirty, sweaty work. But she loved it and she loved being with him.

And then one morning she knew, that for all his efforts to make her feel like more a nuisance than a help, he had come to enjoy her company, too. For some reason, she slept past five. She awoke to see Galen standing in her doorway.

'Did you want to come this morning?' he asked gruffly. She saw past the gruff words. She saw what he did not want her to see. He *wanted* her to be with him.

'Coming,' she answered softly. Where you go, she added to herself, I will follow. She felt a shiver of fear. Of fear and ecstasy. She had just admitted something she wanted very badly not to admit.

Galen honked the horn, the signal that it was time to throw another bale of hay off the tailgate of the truck. They were near the end of the load and Rae pushed the bale along the floor of the truck box with her feet to spare her aching back. Gasping, she cut the twine that held the bale together, and gave it a final shove with her shoulder. The bale tumbled slowly forward, and she gave it one last push—unfortunately her momentum carried her off the end of the truck with the bale.

She lay on the ground, choking with laughter as the truck slammed to a halt and Galen dashed around back.

He bent over her, the concern on his face being replaced with a slow smile when he saw she was laughing.

'Stubborn female,' he said sternly. 'I told you I'd throw the bales while you drove.'

'I drove yesterday.' And poor Galen had nearly been tossed from the truck more than once. She was getting better after a few days of practice with the gears, but her starts were still notoriously jerky.

'You are one of the most uncoordinated people I have ever seen,' Galen said, extending a hand to her.

She took his hand, shaking her head with remorse. 'Stubborn. Uncoordinated. How are we ever going to find me a husband, Galen MacNamara?' It was a light remark intended to distract her from the tantalising tingle of his touch.

A shadow passed over his face, and the eyes that had been laughing became moody. He didn't release her hand, but stood staring down at her.

Her heart's tempo quickened unbearably. By now, she scolded herself, it should know better. She had been working at Galen's side for nearly a week, and these episodes of almost tangible sexual tension between her and Galen were occurring daily—sometimes by the minute. Nothing ever came of it. His face would close up colder than stone and the moment would pass—an unwanted tribute to the tremendous mental and emotional strength and discipline of this man.

Save for those episodes, or, if she was going to be really honest, even slightly enhanced because of them, Rae was enjoying her enforced stay on the farm more than she had ever believed would be possible.

Part of it was that as a writer she had always been particularly sensitive to her surroundings. Here the magic of spring sunshine warmed her soul, the star-encrusted nights filled her with delight. She was enchanted by the scenery, by the animals. The cows followed her every move with large, liquid brown eyes. Birds and squirrels chattered in the trees of the forest groves that rimmed the perimeters of the farm.

Each night she walked alone after dinner. For too long she had avoided moments of solitude, moments of silence, deathly afraid of what they would show her of herself. But instead of revealing a twisted and worthless person—the kind of woman who could be happily taken in by a married man—she was amazed to be discovering she liked her own company, and those moments of introspection that she had avoided and dreaded filled her only with a growing assurance of her own worth.

The patterns of life on the farm also went a long way in soothing her troubled soul. There was so much work to be done every day—h d, relentlessly physical work. And yet, instead of being draining, all the physical activity and fresh air filled her with more energy than she had felt in years, and then allowed her to sleep deeply and dreamlessly at night.

And somehow, without ever really exerting herself, she began to feel wonderfully at home with the irrepressible MacNamara family. Billy was still in daily contact with his teacher and had to keep abreast of assignments, but he still had plenty of free time, and when Rae wasn't with Galen she was with Billy. She watched him ride his horse, and sat in his tree-house with him, and told him bedtime stories.

She sensed Galen's growing trust of her, and though he would never say it she was pretty sure he approved of the time she spent with Billy, especially since Billy seemed to have totally forgotten the original reason why he and Gramps had plotted to get Rae to the farm.

Rae was delighted by the MacNamaras' concerted efforts to spend time together. And not time in front of the television. It had been turned on only once since she'd arrived. Rather, they spent an informal hour or two together every night as a family. They played cards, or board games, worked on a model, or the huge jigsaw set up in one corner of the den, or just talked over steaming mugs of cocoa. Maybe it was because she had never belonged to a normal family that she enjoyed these simple family gatherings so tremendously. She felt a contentment in belonging to and being included in the family circle that was like nothing she had ever felt. It created a warm glow in the bottom of her belly that made her feel calmly and richly satisfied with life. She refused to dwell on the fact that her inclusion was destined to be brief.

But in the end she knew it was one factor more than any other that contributed to the glowing sense of wonder, of contentment, of well-being that she was experiencing. It was the presence of Galen in her life. She found his company invigorating and intriguing. If he was incredibly complex—moody one moment, and mischief-filled the next—it only contributed to his attraction. It was never dull to be around Galen—even if he was on the other side of the room doing nothing more exciting than chewing on an unlit pipe and reading a book. Even then there was a promise of fire in him.

Added to that, he had more depth than any man she had ever known, and getting to know him was like unwrapping layers and layers of tissue paper from some precious object. Each layer offered some surprise, some delight, and yet always there remained the promise of some day unwrapping what was at the core of this magnificent package.

It would take a lifetime to know him, and yet she had the oddest sensation of having always known him. And sometimes his actions that should have surprised her the most, like a sudden unexplained gesture of tenderness, surprised her the least, because she had known all along, somewhere in her heart of hearts, that this was what Galen really was. She was beginning to realise that *real* strength in a man was something more than rippling muscles. It was the ability to be unapologetically gentle and caring, and Galen had that ability.

Her growing sense of self-contentment was helping her to trust herself again. Less and less did she doubt her intuition about Galen. Less and less was she inclined to compare him with Roger, or to make bitter blanket statements about all men. What she felt for Galen, though admittedly her emotion was still constrained, was as different as night from day from what she had felt for Roger. They were, after all, two men as different as night and day. She recognised now that Roger's slick and suave wooing had hidden from her the heart of a conman. He'd been tremendously good at the game he played, but it had always been just that—a game.

Galen, on the other hand, didn't play games. There was an earthy honesty about him that was completely trustable. Even the fact that he could lapse into intimidating remoteness portrayed his deep honesty. He wasn't about to pretend to be feeling friendly and effusive if it wasn't true. That, in the end, was the real difference between him and Roger. One man was completely a pretence and one was completely without it.

Galen's complete integrity made her feel even guiltier about the notes she jotted down in exhaustion at the end of each enormously full day. Sometimes she nearly told him, because she would have loved to have heard his reactions to what she wrote. But mostly the time just never seemed quite right, or his trust seemed too new to put to this kind of test.

I will tell him before I go, she promised herself, and would dismiss it at that.

The only thing that didn't strike her as completely true about Galen was his adamance that he wanted no part of a relationship. If that was true, how could he explain the many moods that danced through his eyes when they rested on her, which was with growing frequency? Sometimes tender, sometimes sad, sometimes smouldering. And yet always in the end his strength won out, and he would back away in denial of what she had seen in his eyes. Afraid of himself, or afraid of her?

Still, if a man tried to tell you he wasn't ready for something, Rae felt it was in the best interests of self-preservation to believe him. And despite her growing feelings of self-esteem and peace of mind—despite the forceful attraction she could not deny she felt for Galen—she wasn't sure she was ready for anything either. And maybe that was why she was enjoying Galen so much. She felt no pressure to try and take the relationship further.

She felt free to just enjoy his company and get to know him. And for the most part, after she'd overcome the barrier of his suspicions about her, that seemed to be exactly how he felt about her as well.

It was as if, in the long days they shared together, they had reached an unspoken agreement that protected them both. An agreement to just keep everything friendly and uncomplicated. And yet, for all that, there was a strange something in both of them that refused to heed the wisdom of the unspoken pact, that would leap unbidden to sizzle in the air between them, to wrest from them their control over the directin of the relation-ship.

Destiny? Rae had asked herself once, dazedly, and then shaken off the thought as too ridiculous to ponder. Some of Gramps' silly, wonderfully leprechaun-like philosophies were rubbing off on her!

She was drawn out of her thoughts, became aware again that she was sprawled in a rather undignified heap in the mud. Galen's strong hands were lift-ing her to her feet. Neither of them showed any inclination to let go once she was safely up.

The moment would pass, she reassured herself raggedly, as it had passed a dozen times before. Galen would blink and the enticing intensity would disappear from those coal-black eyes. Except this time the moment was showing no sign of passing.

His eyes were drinking in her face with a kind of tender hunger.

'Rae,' he finally said, his voice husky and

tormented, 'are you real?'

She heard the true question. Are you all that you appear to be? And in her state of delightfully aggravated tension she answered the question with her heart. 'Yes.'

But, even as the single word tumbled without thought from her lips, she felt a stab of guilt. Was she? And what about those pieces of paper locked up tight within her suitcase? What about her faintly sordid past? Were those lies? Sins of omission? Was that what he meant when he asked if she was all she appeared to be? Or was the question strictly spiritual? If it was, her unhesitating yes was completely honest.

Because here, on this wonderfully isolated island farm, she had unfolded effortlessly into all she could be. She genuinely loved the work and the animals, the domestic scene, and Gramps and Billy and herself. Yes, she was *real*. As real as she had ever been.

Her mental debate over whether to tell all—Rae past and future, as well as present—lasted only seconds, rushing through her mind in a wave that quickly receded back out to sea. For a split second a qualifier framed itself in her mind, but then she let that go, too. This was not the time or the place. Not now, when she was being overwhelmed by his physical presence, when she felt only an animal desire to lose herself completely in this moment. No, this was not the time to debate philosophical issues in her head, and her mind demanded that she empty it, in order to experience completely the sensation of the lips that were dropping rapidly over hers.

Contact. She felt an explosion shudder through

her. Her mind engaged briefly again, telling her she was as surprised as a sixteen-year-old receiving her first kiss. So much of Roger had been pretence—she hadn't even realised how much of her response had been romantic illusion as dictated by the articles in glossy magazines. Dizzily it occurred to her that Roger had not been real—this was real—and then Roger was gone from her mind, she sensed forever. Her mind once again went blank to thought, leaving itself only open to the wondrous and completely captivating sensation of Galen's mouth on hers, of her wildly spontaneous reaction to him. She felt fresh and clean, amazingly as if this were the very first time lips had ever laid claim to hers.

Galen's exploration of her mouth became less tentative and wondering, intensifying and deepening as though he sensed that her hunger and yearning could match his. His tongue flicked into the hollow of her yielding mouth, and its flame flashed through her, racing like wildfire through her veins, suffusing her heart, turning her stomach to jelly, her backbone to putty, her legs to spaghetti.

She collapsed helplessly against him, their two bodies melting together in an inferno of passion. He stoked the fire—gathering her trembling form close in his strong arms, running steely hands with leashed strength up the silken length of her back, over the gently rounded mounds of her bottom.

'Galen,' she protested when his lips left hers, but the protest turned to plea when the familiar heat of his lips seared along the line of her neck, nibbled savagely on an ear, moved into the hollow of her collarbone. 'Galen,' she breathed.

But she could not just take from this man, could

not just be the passive recipient of this experience.
Her moist and heated lips began their own voyage of
bold discovery. She kissed the strong column of his
throat, ran her slightly parted lips slowly over the
hair-roughened texture of his cheeks, pulled him
down so that she might anoint his eyes and his ears,
and then, hungrily, his throat once more.

Of their own volition her hands moved to his
jacket, working the zipper down and then slipping
inside. She ran her hands caressingly over the hard,
compelling surface of his chest, and then her hands
insisted on knowing more. Trembling, she fumbled
with the buttons of his coarse workshirt, one by one
freeing them until her hands reached their objective.
She slipped them inside his shirt to touch with
reverence the heated satin surface of smooth skin
that encased his muscular torso. Her hands explored upward, dancing in the roughness of the hair
that matted his chest in burnished bronze
curls.

'Rae,' he moaned, his voice hoarse with desire,
his own hands beginning their gentle search. Her
jacket came undone, and a shaft of cold air hit her,
and then was dispelled by the searing heat their
mutual discovery was generating. His large, lean
hands made short work of the snap buttons on the
too-large cotton shirt she wore. And then they were
inside, spanning her waist, moving in tender,
exploratory circles up her ribcage. He ran his hands
over the flimsy fabric of lace that was her bra, and
her nipples tautened beneath the command of his
touch. He reached around the back—and then
jerked away with an abruptness that almost sent her
to her knees.

For a second she could only stare at him with

uncomprehending fear and humiliation. Had she done something wrong? Had she been too wanton? Too aggressive? But then she, too, heard the thud of hoofbeats coming up rapidly behind them.

'Oh, dear God,' she muttered, a blush adding yet more heat to her face. Without bothering to do up the buttons of her shirt, she followed Galen's example and quickly tucked in her shirt and did up the zip to her jacket. She spun round to see Billy, looking like a peanut seated on a barrel, galloping towards them. He rode bareback, with an exuberant confidence that she might have appreciated at any other time.

'Oh, the joys of parenthood,' Galen murmured, his hand coming to rest lightly and possessively on her shoulder. She glanced up at him. That small and oh, so casual gesture signalled a subtle change in their relationship. He was not going to attempt to hide what had passed between them from his matchmaker son. Was he unconcerned about the juvenile interpretation? Did he *want* the relationship to break new ground, to go where it had not gone before?

Billy pulled to a halt in front of them, his squirrel-bright eyes taking in the scene with alert and unbridled curiosity. 'Were you guys smooching?' he asked with awed eagerness.

'Aren't you supposed to be doing schoolwork?' Galen asked sternly, wisely ignoring the question.

'It's lunch time, Dad!'

Rae and Galen exchanged startled glances. Neither had been aware of the swift passage of time.

'Dad, were you guys——'

'How would you like to make five bucks, son?'

A greedy light of interest came on in Billy's eyes, though he was obviously torn between pursuing the subject of smooching or his father's offer.

'How could I make five dollars?' he finally asked warily.

'Rent me Sugar for the afternoon.'

'Weak, Galen,' Rae murmured under her breath. 'Very weak.'

Galen glared at her, then looked back at Billy. 'I thought I'd teach Rae how to ride,' he added wickedly, his hand tightening warningly on hers when she started to protest.

'Really? Can I watch?'

'Nope. That's the other part of the deal. You have to leave us alone for the whole afternoon.'

'Can I have the five dollars right now?' Billy asked, sliding from his horse's bare back.

'I think you can trust me for it,' Galen replied. straight-faced.

Billy handed the reins to his father, and watched as Galen catapulted lithely on to the horse's back.

'But you said Rae——'

'Beat it, Billy,' Galen advised softly, holding down a hand for Rae. She took it and managed to scramble up behind Galen. The ground seemed a long way away, but then she wrapped her arms tightly around Galen's waist and her trepidation evaporated.

Billy was grinning up at them with an expression of unsettling knowing. He turned and walked away, his walk quickly breaking into a run.

'Gramps,' he yelled excitedly, though he was well

out of hearing range of the house, 'Gramps!'

Galen smiled and then sighed. 'There goes my parent-of-the-year award. Jeez. I bribed him. I told him to beat it.'

'Plus he's going to think all his matchmaking has paid off,' Rae pointed out quickly, probing tentatively for Galen's feelings.

'Maybe he wouldn't be so far wrong,' Galen replied softly, glancing over his shoulder at her.

The reply warmed her more than the golden spring sunshine that drenched the air around them.

Her arms tightened even more around his waist, and she leaned appreciatively into the strong line of his back, her cheek resting on his shoulder-blade.

'Then again,' Galen said, teasing now, but maybe also a little startled by his own admission, 'what is it they say about spring and a young man's blood?'

'You're not that young,' she informed him, giving him a smart smack on his broad shoulder.

'I'm not that old!' he came back indignantly. 'Besides, you'd have to be nearly dead not to feel something stir within you on a day like this.' His tone softened. 'Can't you feel it, Rae? The earth being reborn, and with it a lightening of the soul? A willingness to be innocent again, to hope again, to dream again? Maybe,' his voice softened so much she had to strain to hear it, 'maybe to try again.'

'Oh, yes,' she whispered, tears pricking at her eyes at the remarkable sensitivity with which he had captured the spirit of this spring day, had articulated her own hazy, golden thoughts.

He nudged the horse with his heels, and the mood changed, though it lost none of its magic. It went from dreamily introspective to laughter-filled as Sugar broke into an ambling trot.

'Ga-Galen,' she managed to protest jerkily, her bottom bouncing about three feet off the horse's back, 'I'm going to fall off!'

'Hold on tighter,' he advised unsympathetically.

Fine for him to say, she thought, her shaky laughter spilling through gritted teeth. He rode like an Indian, his legs wrapped solidly around the horse, his rear seemingly glued to the horse's back even in this choppy gait.

'Ga-Galen!'

He laughed, and it was a wonderful sound as it shimmered across the air. It was a song of freedom, a tribute to man's capacity for joy. And then he nudged the horse again, and in a moment her unbridled laughter joined his.

It was a laughter without reason—a pure bubbling up of joy caused by wind and sunshine, by the enthralling thud of a horse's hooves, by the magnificent strength and rhythm of its movements, by the back pressed hard into her breasts. It was a laughter that worshipped spring.

They thundered across the pasture, the cattle scattering in their path, and then turning to look after them with nearly human expressions of prissy condemnation.

'Galen,' she heard herself gasping. 'Go faster! Please go faster!'

He complied and Sugar sprang to life, flattening out against the ground. Rae squinted over Galen's shoulder, and the wind whipped through her hair,

slapped bright colour into her cheeks, made tears
sting at her eyes and then run, unnoticed, down her
face.

Finally, as they approached the trees at the edge of
the pasture, Galen slowed the horse down. Just in
time, Rae thought, because she was growing weak
from laughter and exertion.

'Watch the branches,' he advised, ducking his
head. The horse picked its way along a narrow forest
path, and the magic mood again softened itself into a
fabric spun with gold.

There were no words between them, for the magic
had carried them to a place where words became
sacrilege, where a different language was spoken
and listened to. It was a language of spirit,
transmitted by touch and by gesture and by eyes
seeking out eyes.

The path narrowed, and Galen slipped off the
horse, looping a rein casually over a bare branch.
He held out his arms, and Rae slid into them.
Silently, their hands fitting together as naturally as
two interlocking pieces from a puzzle, they walked
for a long while, still without words, still not needing
words. Rae knew from the look on his face that he
was drinking in the scent of the earth, listening to the
crunch of long dead leaves beneath their feet, filling
his every sense with the world and with her. With
the touch of her hand in his, with the way her eyes
came to rest on his face.

Finally he stopped, reached up and ran a gentle
finger over a tree branch.

'Look, Rae,' he said softly.

At first she saw nothing. A tree branch, twisted
and bare from winter and mingled with other tree
branches to make a cobwebby portrait of winter's

starkness. But then she saw what his fingers touched with such gentle reverence, and she stood on tiptoes, stretching until she too could feel the soft velvet of a bud. A tiny, furry bud showing only the faintest of green—and yet in that colour the promise that winter had ended. Their hands touched, intertwined, and they went on.

But her eyes were open now, and she could see it all through the glade. Winter's end. Fragile stems of green grass poking through the brown overlay. Buds preparing to burst forward with colour and life. Tiny, hearty crocuses pushing up defiantly through the crusty, gloomy shell winter had spread over the land.

Galen let go of her hand, searched his pocket, and came out with a penknife. With slow deliberation he inspected the huge gnarled trunk of a fir tree. Then he made the first cut—a sure white line springing from the grey of the trunk. The line shaped itself into a heart, and then into two names.

Galen and Rae.

She laughed. She threw herself into his arms, and covered his face with kisses. The ice within her groaned under an unbearable burden, groaned and then gave way. Spring had finally come.

Later, from far away, she heard the sound of a truck, felt Galen break the bond of her lips.

'Another myth about the country life,' he said drily. 'I think we'd have more privacy if we were in Times Square . . . and if that's Gramps, there's going to be hell to pay.'

'I didn't even know there was a road,' she murmured, her eyes fastened on his lips with unabashed hunger.

He nodded over her shoulder. 'It's right there.

The road to Clarice's.'

She recognised the truck as the one belonging to
Clarice. It slowed when Clarice spotted them, and
then was gone by in a flash. But in that flash Rae
had seen something in Clarice's eyes that made her
shiver, as though winter had abruptly returned.

She tried to shake the feeling by seeking the
warmth of Galen's eyes. Her shiver became a chill.
Because, though he had made no move to let her go,
his eyes were not on her. They rested instead on the
dust the truck was leaving in its wake, a perturbed
and troubled light replacing the pure sunshine that
had danced in them only moments before.

Galen made no attempt to pick up where they had
left off. He seemed remote now, preoccupied. Even
the ride back to the barn held none of its former joy.

And that night, he announced abruptly after
dinner that he had to go out for a while. Rae felt
something very like panic claw at her throat. Who
knew better than she that there was only one place
for him to go?

CHAPTER NINE

GALEN stood in his darkened bedroom gazing out at a moon-washed night. He could make out the skeleton of the new bridge. It would be another three or four days before they could drive across it, according to Ralph. It was already overdue. Somehow Galen couldn't bring himself to care, though he had work to begin in the fields across the creek. He supposed he could phone out and hire somebody, if it came to that. In his own inspection of the bridge earlier today, it hadn't looked as if it was going to be ready in three or four days.

He knew he should be riding Ralph a little more about it, and he knew he wouldn't. It was as if, in the last two weeks, he'd lived on an enchanted island—pleasantly isolated from the rest of the world. Isolated from the world, from grim realities, from the heartache of truth.

Truth was that people did not fall in love—did not feel so strongly—in such a short span of time as he and Rae had. The isolation had made everything speed up, had given their relationship an intensity it would not otherwise have had. Truth was that an odd set of circumstances had pushed them together. When those circumstances changed, returned to normal, would there be anything left? No. She would cross back over that bridge and the enchanted illusion would be shattered.

His eyes caught on his own reflection in the

window. He looked younger, he thought, younger, more carefree, happier than he had in years. She had come, like a woodland nymph, waved a wand, and given him back things he thought he would never feel again. She had given him the gift of youth and of love, but he felt an unspoken time-limit—connected with that bridge.

Because, for all that he felt better than he had in years, he could not quite make himself believe it was real, that it could last. Too many years of cynicism under his belt, he supposed, too many years of habitual scoffing at romance to be entirely swept away by what he was feeling. Yes, the bridge would be finished, and it would be over—this too-brilliant-to-be-believed period in his life. And maybe it was just as well. The memories of these weeks would mellow and warm him forever. This fairy-tale didn't have to become tainted by reality—love being swallowed whole by the dragon of bitter battles and shrewish fighting matches, disillusionment and mistrust.

A splash of colour illuminated the trees just down from his room, and he realised she still had her bedroom light on. He frowned. Night after night her light glowed on the trees until late. When he'd asked her about it, she'd seemed vague and secretive. Or had she? Was that only him, reading everything through the lens of his wariness, his cynicism?

A picture of her crowded his mind, washing away the thoughtful scowl. How she had changed from the reserved, haunted woman he had first seen!

In his mind's eye he could see her now, in too-large men's clothes, that made her look spunky,

ready for anything, and more feminine than the law
should allow. He could picture her looking at him
with those wide, shining sapphire eyes, and that
heartbreaking smile and that expression of pure
wonder.

Other pictures crowded his mind—of Rae with
her head thrown back in laughter, cuddling a kitten,
reaching solemnly and timidly to pat a shy calf's
nose. Of her seated on Sugar for the first time by
herself; glaring down at the truck's gearshift with
tongue between teeth; sitting on the edge of Billy's
bed. And then of the way she felt in his arms, the
way her lips felt on his, or when they anointed his
throat and eyes and ears with such wonder. The
pictures filled him with an aching tenderness that
wouldn't be dispelled by his gruff reminder that
eventually it all boiled down to demands and dirty
socks.

It could be different with her. The renegade
thought blasted through his mind, refused to be
ignored. She was such a different person from Sara.
It was the thought he had avoided scrupulously. So
far he had taken each moment, accepted it as a gift,
but looked for no more, tried to see no further. And
now that he had taken that one small and tentative
step into the future, he knew he had made the most
dangerous mistake of his life. Now there was no
going back. With a groan of defeat, of ecstasy, he
turned from his window, yanked open his door, and
went quietly down the hall to her room. He heard a
shuffling of papers when he knocked at the door, but
when he entered he didn't see any papers, not even a
magazine. The murky suspiciousness of his thoughts
was erased by the tender welcome in her smile, by
the way she was dressed.

'Hi,' she greeted him softly. 'I couldn't sleep. I feel restless.' It was only partly true. The other part she had just stuffed guiltily under the bed. She refused to linger on the guilt, let it taint a moment with Galen. She was going to tell him, after all. Besides, he had secrets, too. Though their relationship had forged ahead, he had not told her why he had gone to see Clarice the other night.

'Unfinished business,' he had said, without elaborating, and she, having no wish to play an irrationally jealous woman, had had to content herself with that. Besides, his every look, his every gesture, assured her that Clarice, if she had ever played a romantic role in his life, did no longer. She was convinced that that was all he had gone to tell the other woman that night.

She reached for her short, blue satin housecoat, and threw it casually over the brief, white silk teddy she was wearing. She felt oddly unembarrassed to have been caught in such a state of undress. In fact, she was glad he had seen her like this—long-legged, slender, and utterly feminine. Too often he saw her in ridiculously large clothes that she felt made her look like a circus clown.

She saw a light of appreciation go on in his eyes just before she turned to the window, and she smiled a happy, secret smile. He looked at her with the very same fire burning in his eyes no matter how she was dressed. It made her feel wonderful—cherished and desired for what he saw within her and not for all the trappings.

Yet, except for a few breathless kisses, a few endless embraces, theirs had not been a physical love. And lately Rae yearned with a burning desire

for all that they felt for each other to move into that
one unexplored dimension between them—a joyous
confirmation of the long looks and the liquid
laughter they shared. A wordless way of saying in
yet one more magnificent way what they had been
saying wordlessly to each other for days.

'I'm restless, too,' he said, joining her at the
window, one hand finding its way casually to her
hair, running lightly through it. 'Do you feel like
going for a walk? Maybe the fresh air and exercise
will wear us out'

She joined him a few minutes later outside. It was
a beautiful night—silver-washed by a bright moon,
kissed by a million dancing stars.

He tucked her arm through his, and they walked
in the comfortable quiet of people who had come to
treasure each other and did not need desperately to
fill gaps of silence with chatter.

And yet, for all that the silence was an easy and
companionable one, something else tingled
alluringly in the air between them. His thumb made
small and intimate circles within the palm of her
hand, and she knew he was as acutely aware of the
intriguing tension as she was. Aware of a sizzling
expectation that the time was ripe for that unnamed
something to blossom between them.

She shivered at the sudden intrusion in her
tranquillity of a raging desire to feel his lips, his
hands, his body.

'Are you cold?' he asked with soft concern. 'We'll
slipo into the barn for a minute.'

The barn wasn't heated, and yet it was amazing
how warm it was kept by the body heat of the
animals inside. Rae, shaken by her ever-present and
growing need, let go of his hand and walked over

to Sugar. She rubbed the furry forehead affectionately, and some of her tranquillity returned.

How far I've come, she thought, remembering how timid this giant, gentle animal had first made her. She sighed. 'I love it,' she whispered, lost within herself.

Galen came up behind her and moved to her side. She meant it, he realised, watching her as those huge, expressive eyes roamed the rough-hewn interior of the barn. And yet he also recognised a sadness in her that had not been there before.

She was saying goodbye, he deduced. Like him, she could not quite believe in happiness. Like him, she was asking nothing more than this moment—planning no future.

And suddenly he recognised the truth. He could not let her go. Somewhere along the path they had travelled together for the past few weeks he had begun to believe in a new truth. A truth based in hope, and not in cynicism, past hurts, the world's rigidly defined rules of what love was, and how long it took for it to happen, and whom it could happen to.

'Don't look so sad,' he implored her softly, touching her cheek.

She turned and gave him a smile, world-weary and wise. 'I just don't want anything to change, and I know it has to.'

How accurately that mirrored his own tormented and twisted thoughts that night. His finger traced the high line of her cheekbone tenderly. A tear slid down, and he caught it and placed it to his lips.

'Maybe it doesn't.'

Rae's eyes widened on his face, and she saw what he meant in his eyes, saw it, and yet was afraid to believe it.

'You don't have to leave when the bridge is done.'

She turned abruptly away from him, and he knew he had disappointed her. And disappointed himself. It wasn't what he had meant to say, and yet some vestige of suspicion, of caution, had reared its ugly head.

He put his hands on her shoulders, spun her gently around, cupped her face in his hands. In the glittering blue of her eyes he found the courage to say what he wanted.

'You don't ever have to leave.'

Another shadow of pain crossed her face and knifed through his heart. What exactly was he offering? To keep her? To have her here as a houseguest for the rest of her life? To eventually woo her into his bed and make her his lifelong mistress?

And then he knew that was not what he wanted. It would be easy and riskless to accept that, and yet it would cheapen what they were meant to be—maybe even prevent them from ever attaining the heights they had the potential to attain together if the circumstances were right. If they were committed.

'Rae, I want you to marry me'

The words came out strong and sure, and he felt suddenly strong and sure. He felt as fully alive as he had ever felt. And his reward was the light that came on in that death-white face. A light so brilliant with love that it nearly blinded him. A light so warm with

love that it took what was left of those wounds inside
of him, closed them over, healed them completely.

He went to her, lifted her easily into strong,
certain arms, and without hesitation carried her up
the ladder to the loft.

'Villain,' she accused playfully when he produced a
sleeping-bag and pillow, and spread them out on
mounds of sweet-smelling hay. 'You've been
plotting this.'

'Billy camps out up here sometimes in the
summer,' he informed her, reaching for her and
pulling her down beside him. 'But I can't claim
complete innocence—I have imagined a moment
very like this one a thousand times since we
met.'

She knelt in the hay beside him, studying him
with unabashed admiration, with eyes so hungry for
the sight of him that she thought it would take a
hundred years of looking at him to fill her up, to
make her feel satisfied. He returned her gaze, and
she felt a sweet joy swelling up within her and
washing over her. It was so evident that he felt as
strongly as she did. Her imagination was playing no
part in this one—no, her imagination was not even
capable of conjuring up such tenderness as she saw
in his darkened, suede eyes.

They had been building towards this moment
since the very first time destiny had pulled them
together, and, now that it had arrived, there was a
strange lack of urgency in it. No, this was not a
moment to be rushed, but rather an experience to be
explored languidly, each second of it slowly
savoured like a fine wine, or an Old Master's
painting . . . or a spring morning's dawn.

They feasted their eyes, and then slowly he reached for her, compelling her down into the soft bed of hay. He touched her with featherlight, worshipping fingertips, caressing her brow, her eyes, her cheekbones, her lips. And then his lips tenderly followed the path his fingers had mapped.

Fingers again, his eyes on her face registering each faint nuance of her reaction as he moved downwards, his strong fingers lingering appreciatively on her neck, her collarbone, her shoulders, and finally her breasts, the nipples already taut and aching with wanting. He unbuttoned her shirt wordlessly and gently, then let his eyes drink of her. And then, once again, his lips followed the course charted by his fingers and his smouldering eyes.

Rae felt what she had felt the first time he had kissed her. Clean and fresh, so glad that something within her had warned her to wait. To wait for precisely the right man and the right moment before she gave over the gift of her body in joyous confirmation of the line in the wedding ceremony that said, 'With my body, I thee worship.'

'Galen,' she whispered hoarsely, desperate to begin her own exploration.

Gently he pinned her questing arms to her sides. 'Let me know you,' he whispered, continuing on his tantalising journey over her most secret places.

Rae obeyed, drifting on a cloud of supreme happiness. She felt as if she was lying on a beach, the gentle lapping of the waves on sand building to a crescendo as a storm moved in. Gentle swells changed slowly and exquisitely to cresting waves and then to crashing breakers.

Finally, she could remain docile no longer and her hands moved to him, tugging from him the barrier of clothing that separated the heated surfaces of their skin. A gasp of pure appreciation escaped her when he was finally free of clothing.

He was magnificent. His body was incredibly hard and lean, nut-brown, gleaming with shimmering diamonds of perspiration. She put her lips to him, and her senses groaned under the weight of stimuli. The way he looked, his taste, his aroma, combined to swamp her senses, almost too much heaven to bear. Tenderly, restraining all in her that begged for immediate release from the soft and sweet tension that had built in those waves within her, she came to know him with her eyes and lips and fingertips.

Only when they had taken each of their senses to the limit, explored endlessly with sight and sound and smell, did the tempo change again. The waves of sensual pleasure now engulfed her completely—foaming white within her, roaring and crashing against the midnight sky of her head.

'Rae.' His voice was hoarsened with his own need, and yet in its questioning tone she heard the note that confirmed his love, his respect for her, his desire that this be an experience that they were both equally eager for so that they chould share completely in the intoxicating heights they had been climbing so rapturously towards.

Tears of joy welled up in her eyes.

'Yes, Galen,' she whispered, and then, a moment later, 'Oh, yes!'

*   *   *

The folds of the sleeping-bag tucked securely around them, they lay tangled possessively together in the hay, not sleeping, not speaking either. They drifted in a world of absolute tranquillity. Galen's hand tenderly and unconsciously stroked Rae's upper arm and shoulder.

She was lying so that she could look at him, and he looked incredible in the slivers of moonlight that illuminated the chiselled features of his face. She shivered in the pure delight of being loved by such a man, and his reverie broke.

He looked down at her, his eyes lingering appreciatively before he spoke. 'Are you cold?'

'That's a question that got me in trouble in the first place,' she responded with husky lightness.

He pulled her closer none the less, his dark eyes continuing to scan her face. 'Trouble?' he teased softly.

'An unfortunate choice of phrase,' she agreed with a sigh of pure contentment. She grew serious. 'I feel as if I've just touched the stars. Nothing like this has ever happened to me before.'

'And nothing quite like this has ever happened to me,' he returned softly, running a wondering fingertip over the moon's silver highlight of her cheekbone. 'It's as if I was told water was wine, and had accepted a cheap imitation as the real thing. Until now. I feel so totally happy. Not so long ago I'd given up on ever feeling totally whole or totally happy again.'

'Why, Galen?'

He tried to shrug it off, but the clearness of his dark eyes clouded. 'It happened a long time ago. It's got nothing to do with you and me. Besides, isn't the first commandment of new love ''thou shall not talk about old heartaches"'?'

'Galen, if some old experience contributed in
making you what you are today, in this moment,
then it does have something to do with you and me.
As for the rule of love, I have a sneaking suspicion
that you and I are going to make our own as we go
along.'

He realised he hadn't actually acknowledged the
burden he carried around within him, until now.
Until she reached out and offered to lighten a load he
suddenly recognised as oppressively heavy. And still
he hesitated. No one had ever known his innermost
soul. His deepest feelings. Not even to Gramps had
he revealed the true extent of his anguish over Sara's
betrayal, Sara's lies. No, he had pretended it hardly
mattered, but suddenly he wanted nothing more
than what Rae offered—release from pretence. He
wanted Rae to know him, to know there was a limit
to his strength, to know he bled when he was cut,
wept inwardly, if never outwardly, when something
he'd believed in with his whole heart and soul had
gone sour, and worse, had turned out not to have
been worth believing in in the first place.

'It's about Billy's mother, isn't it?' she
encouraged.

He turned startled eyes to her, and then smiled
softly. Ah, he would have to remember
that—remember he would never be able to keep
secrets from the astute and perceptive, sensitive
and gentle eyes that rested so compellingly on his
face.

'Her name was Sara,' he began, and then
faltered. Where to begin? Old hurts were welling up
within him already. Maybe it was best, after all, to
leave this buried.

'Tell me.' Her voice was soothing, like a sudden breeze on a torrid summer night.

He took a deep breath. Yes. It was time to lance the wound that festered within.

'We met at university. I was taking an agricultural course. She was taking whatever struck her fancy that term. She was beautiful, as fragile as a porcelain doll. Her hair, blacker than crow's wings, her complexion as white as fresh-fallen snow, her eyes huge and violet and innocent. Or I thought I saw innocence.

'There was so much of her I would only know later, but at first she seemed to be my secret fantasy come true. Loving, gentle, full of laughter and fun and life. She bowled me over the first time she batted her lashes at me. I'm afraid I was every bit the naïve, bumpkin farmer that's so frequently caricatured. I was enthralled with her big-city sophistication, and honoured that she seemed to have taken such a liking to me.

'When she offered me everything, I greedily took it, never ever considering she might be motivated by something other than love, that she might have a motive deeper and darker. I never spotted the desperation in her. I took her at face value and so I didn't understand that she had deliberately escalated things to a point they never would have reached if I'd stayed in control instead of idolising her. Anyway, she bartered—her body for the future—and she won. But I'm getting ahead of myself.

'When I found out that she was pregnant, I was thrilled. I didn't care that she'd told me she was on the Pill and she wasn't. It didn't bother me that I'd have to sacrifice my education. I missed the farm. I wanted to go home. I felt ready for a wife and a family. I still didn't understand.

'But I started to understand three minutes after I'd said, "I do". I was with her when she called her mother. She said, with insulting triumph, "Mama, I married a millionaire."

'I was stunned. I shouldn't have been. I'd known from the beginning that she was fascinated by wealth, by money. It was a fault I managed to overlook, or rationalise. Maybe I even played up to it a bit because I wanted to win her so badly. I bragged about flying my own plane. I flashed around more money than I really had. I told her about how prosperous the farm was. I desperately wanted this exquisite creature to love me—but I never guessed that my playing her game meant that it wasn't me she was falling in love with.

'Later I would find out how desperate she had been. She came from a dirt-poor family. The whole bunch of them saw her looks and style as their ticket out. She was at university on a scholarship—one that she was in danger of losing because she was so frantically shopping for a rich husband that she never applied herself to her studies.

'She found me. I don't think I was what she was looking for, but time was running out for her. I mentioned, to my shame probably more than once, that the farm was worth over a million. It was—is—the land, livestock, machinery, buildings. What I didn't mention was that, while we might have been asset-rich, like most farmers, we were cash-poor. I don't mean we couldn't eat—but we weren't holidaying on the Riviera, either. We lived a simple life.

'You should have seen her face when she first saw

the farm. We had the old house at the time—a big, white clapboard thing that needed paint and looked as if it was going to fall down. I thought she was going to cry.

'And then it started. She needed money for clothes. She wanted money for her mama. Why couldn't we go out and eat more often? Why couldn't we go dancing three times a week? Couldn't we go to Phoenix for the winter the way our neighbours were doing?

'I think it hurt the worst when she started nagging me to sell the farm. But still, for all that, I never lost hope that she'd come around. That she'd mature, and come to feel about the land the way I did.

'I believed strongly in marriage. I meant those words "for better or for worse", and was determined to do everything in my power to make it work. I compromised and took her to Hawaii for a couple of weeks. I indulged her whim for clothes, I forced myself to try and share her interests by taking her out to dance and to eat. I kept hoping that maybe she really loved me a little bit. I thought part of her moodiness and irritability might be because of the pregnancy. I thought maybe things could be all right between us once the baby was born—that she'd be more willing to settle down, to give farm life an honest try.

'Anyway, needless to say, the baby's being born solved not a thing. She rejected Billy completely—just the way sometimes a ewe will reject its lamb. She got wilder than ever. She started going out without me, taking off for days at a time.

'One day she just didn't come back. She'd found

what she wanted—some high roller to take her to the
Riviera. And as it turned out, that didn't fill the
emptiness in her as she'd expected either. I'd hear
about her from time to time—about her wild
escapades, her insatiable thirst for bigger and bigger
thrills. She died of a cocaine overdose about a year
after she'd left.'

His voice turned to a soft growl. 'In retrospect,
it's so easy to say it was a mistake from the
beginning and I never loved her. That it was an
infatuation and that's all. But on the other hand, I
can't believe it was completely hopeless. I think as
she grew older she might have come around. I still
feel an incredible anger with the man who took
her—he knew she was married. But instead of seeing
that as a hands-off signal, he took it as some perverse
kind of challenge. And you know, Sara wasn't all
bad. With time and love and patience—but he
offered her an alternative, and she took it.
Sometimes I'd get the saddest little letters from her,
remembering the farm with something that
approached fondness, asking after Billy. I always
thought some day she'd come back. And my
wedding vows meant enough to me that I knew I'd
be waiting.'

He looked up from the hands he was knotting and
unknotting. Rae was looking at him, her eyes wide
with understanding and shared pain. He felt lighter
than he had in years. The pain of the betrayal
was over, and somehow in the telling of the tale
he had forgiven Sara—a step he had never made before.

He folded Rae into his arms. He was ready for

new beginnings now. With her. With this woman who was everything she appeared to be—and possibly more.

CHAPTER TEN

IT WAS dawn when they walked back towards the house. The night they had shared had been beautiful beyond belief. Rae felt more gloriously alive than she had ever felt. The future glowed with soft promise of more of the same, plus she was going to spend the rest of her life tramping the far reaches of this farm with her hand clasped solidly in Galen's, as it was now. She was going to be his partner, his soulmate, his lover. They were going to have children together. She was finally going to have the family of her dreams.

She had never believed anything so wonderful could happen to her. It seemed like something you read about in a book—a chance in a million, like winning a lottery or being offered a trip to the moon. She felt like an ordinary person who had been welcomed into the domain of the gods.

Galen nudged her. 'Tell me about that beautiful smile.'

'I was just thinking . . . about a family.' She turned shy and wide eyes to him. 'Galen, you do want more children, don't you?'

He hesitated, and her heart caught in her throat. 'About a dozen,' he informed her thoughtfully.

Her laughter pealed across the pink and purple-washed sky. 'A dozen?' she chided playfully.

'OK. But at least three. We need a little brother for Billy, and a girl who looks just like you. And then

she'll need a little sister to play with and to keep the
boys from ganging up on her . . .'

He stopped, took her shoulders and looked deep
into her eyes. 'Do you know what a gift it is even to
be talking like this? You've given me back dreams I
held so deep inside me, I didn't even know they were
still there. Dreams of having a companion to share
my life with, someone who will turn the most
ordinary day into something special to anticipate
and look forward to. Dreams of more children racing
over the far reaches of this farm—of me leading
them around on ponies, and kissing bruised fingers,
and chopping down a Chrismas tree and dragging it
home behind the horse. I don't think I'd realised what a world of grey I inhabited until you
came along and the colour started to seep back
in.'

'Like spring,' she whispered, her eyes wide and
misty on his softened features. 'It's as if spring is
washing away all the starkness of winter, replacing it
with pastel colours and sunshine.'

'Yes,' he agreed warmly, 'exactly like that.'

'When are we going to tell Billy and Gramps?' she
asked as they walked on. 'I'm a little nervous about
that. You know, it's one thing for a little boy to
fantasise about a make-believe mother. The reality
is quite another. For the first time in his life, he'll be
sharing you. I can't live up to all his expectations,
either. They're too pie-in-the-sky. Right now he
probably thinks I never get angry, bake chocolate
cookies almost constantly——'

'Shh, Rae. It'll be fine. Billy and Gramps fell in
love with you from the very first. Actually, I think I
probably did too, but I was too stubborn to admit
it.'

'Oh, and I love them both, too,' she said
earnestly, 'and did almost from the start. You know,
I used to think Gramps was quite hilarious with all
his superstitious talk of destiny. But how else could
these four people who felt such a strong and instant
pull towards one another have ended up together
against such odds?'

'I don't think you need to worry about being a
mother to Billy,' Galen assured her. 'There was
such a natural and strong affinity between you from
the beginning. I'm not saying there won't be some
adjustments to make, but with genuine caring I
think everything will work out tremendously. And
you'll have to remember you're in a house full of
Irishmen. A few fights here and there are the
norm. Even you and I are going to squabble
occasionally.'

'I find that hard to believe,' she deadpanned
demurely. After their first few days together she
could see that, yes, there would be spats and
arguments from time to time. But she also saw that
as a sign of a healthy, three-dimensional
relationship. People living together didn't always
agree. That would be part of getting to know each
other, and she wanted to know *all* of Galen. She
wanted to know how he dealt with anger and upsets,
as well as good times and laughter. She believed a
fight, properly handled, and worked through until
the end, could strengthen a relationship rather than
weaken it.

They walked in thoughtful silence for a bit, and
then he spoke again. 'So Gramps and Billy won you
over right away. When did you fall for me?'

'Well, I don't know,' she teased. 'Certainly not at
first meeting. Good God—who could fall for such a

rude and bristling giant?'

Galen threw back his head and laughed, then became more sombre. 'I guess I sensed the danger you posed to me almost right away, and fought it only because I didn't understand it could be real.'

She laughed softly. 'I guess maybe I sensed the danger right away, too, Galen. Because I think I started to fall for you the moment I saw the picture of you that Gramps and Billy sent me. Not that I could admit it at the time—I only knew I found the stranger in that photograph so intriguing that I felt compelled to look at his picture again and again. I think perhaps a part of my heart recognised you, and knew you would be the man I'd be spending the rest of my life with.'

Galen mulled that over before answering. 'You know, I think hearts do recognise something, as bizarre as that may seem to someone who hasn't experienced it. Because even at first, when I was determined to see you as an intruder—as a foolish young woman stupid enough and shallow enough to answer an ad for a husband—I sensed the sadness in you, and I had to fight my heart's need to offer you comfort.' He paused. 'You haven't told me yet what put that sadness in your eyes, and it certainly isn't there any more, so I won't even push you. But when you're ready, I want to help you be free of any burdens from your past—just as you've given me freedom from mine.'

She touched his arm. 'Thank you,' she said simply, for now offering nothing more. Yes, some day she would have to tell him about Roger. Some day very soon. It was only fair that he know the darkest part of her past before they married. And yet love was new to her. She wanted to bask in it for

just a while longer. She wanted to enjoy its freshness
and newness for a little bit more. She wanted it to
show her it was not fragile or easily shattered. When
her confidence in this beautiful new experience had
grown, then she would expose it to an ugly truth.
Two ugly truths. Well, maybe the second was not so
ugly. His reaction to her being a writer couldn't be
any worse than him seeing her as stupid and
shallow. She smiled inwardly. She would make him
a gift of that article. An engagement gift, leaving a
little piece of herself here with him, when she
returned to Calgary to straighten out her affairs.

And the truth about Roger could wait, too. The
time was not right. Not right now, when she knew
how strongly Galen felt about marriage, about his
own wife's infidelity, and about the man who had
taken her in adultery. It made Rae unsure how to
admit that she, too, however unwittingly, had done
something he would deplore.

'When you're ready, Rae,' he reassured her
gently, reading her face, and she felt a quiver of pure
delight that she had been lucky enough to meet
another human being capable of such sensitivity to
her feelings.

She would know when the time was right, she told
herself firmly, and then she could choose her words
with care. She had been naïve—a victim of wanting
something too much. Wanting what she had now.
But only now was she wise enough to know that it
couldn't be forced, or imagined. It just was.

'Didn't you promise to make Billy waffles this
morning?' Galen asked, and she knew he was trying
to lighten her mood, and she felt almost dizzy for
loving him.

'I did—and I'd better get at it.'

'We'll stuff him full of waffles, and then give him the news. He'll probably think he's died and gone to heaven—waffles and a mommy on the same morning.' He kissed her lingeringly. 'Speaking of having died and gone to heaven . . .' he whispered against her hair.

Rae and Galen laughed like children who had been allowed to play Santa's elves as they prepared breakfast together. They were unapologetically romantic, licking cream off the ends of each other's fingertips, feeding each other strawberries, touching and cuddling at the slightest excuse.

'I think we'll make this a tradition,' Galen murmured from behind her, his arms wrapped around her waist as she tried valiantly to concentrate on making waffle-batter. 'Sunday will always be waffle day, and you and I will always make waffles together. Agreed?'

'Agreed,' she said, trying to remember how much flour she'd added while Galen nuzzled her ear. 'As long as I'm left out of the tradition of marching through the house at an ungodly hour, making an unholy noise——'

'No way!' he said, with mock sternness. 'When you're a MacNamara, I'll expect you to sing about it.'

'Well, since you put it that way—for heaven's sake, Galen, you just made me drop an egg!'

'I didn't do anything,' he protested.

'I know. You *stopped* doing that lovely thing to my ear.'

'My name is MacNamara,' he crooned while he nibbled her ear.

'Your name is mud,' she said sadly, as the second egg slipped through her fingers . . .

They decided to make it a special occasion, and
set the huge oak table in the dining-room with
antique lace and fine china. They even added
candles. Finally, they allowed Billy and Gramps to
come downstairs.

The pair sensed that something was in the air, and
though Billy was obviously chomping at the bit to
know what *exactly* it was, Rae suspected Gramps had
coached him to keep his questions to himself. The
atmosphere around the table was festive as they
devoured waffles, whipped cream and strawberries.

Billy, with his mouth full of waffles, suddenly
uttered a hair-curling expletive.

The rest of them looked at him in stunned
astonishment.

'Since when do we use language like that?' Galen
finally asked sternly.

'Since *she's* here,' Billy muttered
unapologetically, his eyes fastened on the dining-
room window.

As one, all eyes turned to the window. Gramps
muttered a curse that put Billy's to shame. Rae did
the same, if silently. She could feel the perfection she
had expected of this day marred by the woman
strolling out of the trees and coming up the drive.

She wondered if she had forgotten how attractive
Clarice was, or just managed not to think about it.
Now she felt intimidated. There was no vestige of a
farmer remaining. Clarice wore a white lamb's-wool
jacket, black slacks, smart shoes. She walked with
the grace and confidence of a model, the glamour
she exuded being reinforced by the cloud of
platinum-blonde hair that floated around a face that
would have had to be called handsome, rather than
beautiful, but that all the same was forcefully

attractive.

'Yoo hoo,' she called, waving towards the window.

Rae decided she *hated* people who said 'yoo hoo.'

Galen's features revealed nothing as he tossed down his napkin and went to the door. He didn't look happy to see her, but then he didn't look unhappy either.

For heaven's sake, Rae chided herself. Clarice was a neighbour—she was going to be *their* neighbour. She had better get used to her dropping by without feeling this dreadful tug of insecurity at the bottom of her belly. She trusted Galen. She was over the wounds Roger had so callously inflicted. Wasn't she?

Clarice entered the room with understated, and yet unmistakably dramatic, flair. Rae could have sworn a chilly breeze came in with her—or maybe it was only the icy, measuring look in the cool jade eyes that rested on her, and did not reflect the poised smile on wide, sensuous lips.

'Why, hello, Kyle. Billy. Rae.' Her eyes lingered on Rae with a kind of brutal satisfaction that made Rae shiver. The phrase 'a wolf in sheep's clothing' leapt spontaneously to mind, and it had nothing to do with Clarice's jacket. Rae watched her warily, trying to reassure herself that Clarice could do nothing to hurt her. The woman didn't even know her, for God's sake.

'May I join you?' Without waiting for an answer, she took the chair at the opposite end of the table to Galen's.

Was she laying down territorial rights? Rae wondered. The chair would have seemed most appropriate for the woman of the house. Which is

going to be me, she reminded herself baldly to shore
up her flagging confidence.

'How come you're here?' Billy asked with naked
hostility. Rae felt sorry for him. He had known, with
his childish intuition, that something special was
going to happen this morning. And with his childish
intuition, perhaps he sensed some vague threat, just
as she herself did.

Galen threw him a warning look. 'Did you want
to join us for breakfast, Clarice?'

She looked at the heaped plates carefully and then
shook her head, her demeanour both amused and
superior. 'I think not. Goodness, all that sugar! It's
not good for a child who tends to be a little
hyperactive.' The look she gave Rae spoke volumes.
It accused her of being like the wicked witch in
Hansel and Gretel, using sugar to win the hearts of
unsuspecting children. 'Perhaps a coffee?' Clarice
suggested, shivering delicately. 'It might take the
chill off.'

The coffee was on the sideboard directly behind
her. She made no attempt to help herself, and Galen
moved over and got her a coffee before sitting down
again. Rae felt a tingle of jealousy mingle with her
wariness. Galen certainly never got her coffee.

She made herself look at him, wanting to be
reassured that the world they shared had not been
shattered by the arrival of this hostile and beautiful
intruder. To her hopeful eyes, Galen seemed
somewhat less than enraptured by the appearance of
the woman at the end of the table. In fact, his eyes
met Rae's and he winked at her broadly.

Rae smiled back, a touch tremulously, and then
noticed that Clarice was watching them, her eyes
narrowed with a baleful, catlike coldness.

She's moving in for the kill, Rae deduced uneasily when those feline eyes sought her face. Why do I feel I'm in competition with this horrible woman? Rae asked herself savagely. Galen had proposed to *her*, not Clarice. The silent war being waged between herself and Clarice should be over—should be non-existent, in fact—and yet her every instinct alerted her to the fact that Clarice was drawing up battle lines. She was further warned, by the sheer and malevolent craft in Clarice's eyes, that her arsenal was going to be huge and lethal.

Why, I'm being ridiculous, Rae informed herself sternly. She reminded herself that she didn't know this woman. And unless Clarice had been prowling around the house, snooping under the beds, her secrets were safe.

Rae cast Clarice a glance intended to confirm her thoughts. But what it did was show her a woman who possessed a certain mysterious allure, a potent sexuality, and the strength of self-command. And Billy and Gramps had been worried about her power over Galen, Rae remembered, her uneasiness returning full strength.

Clarice was smiling smoothly at her. 'Rae, I was just fascinated by the fact that you worked for a magazine. So do you know what I did? I called *Womanworld* and booked a subscription.'

Rae felt herself stiffen.

'When I called I just happened to mention I had met somebody who worked in the advertising department. Can you imagine my surprise when I was told you didn't work in the advertising department at all? That it had been *years* since you worked in the advertising department?'

Rae felt herself freeze. What a wicked opponent

this was! This was it, then. The cards were going to
be laid on the table.

'Oh?' Rae asked, sheer force of will allowing her
to seem only mildly surprised.

'Why, Galen, didn't you even know that your
guest is quite illustrious? She's considered one of the
best feature writers in the business.' Clarice paused.
'Or at least she was, until last year. Something to do
with a married man, I believe.'

Rae felt the blood drain from her face. She felt she
was being sucked alive into the suffocating black
cloud of her worst nightmare. This couldn't be
happening. Nobody at *Womanworld* would have told
a complete stranger something like that over the
phone.

Please wake up, she thought frantically, turning
panic-stricken eyes to Galen. Her nightmare
intensified, clawing at her, pulling her deeper into
its horrible yawning vortex. Words of pleading and
explanation raced through her head, but they came
in twisted snatches, and the look in his eyes killed
her voice. Her heart. Her dreams.

She looked out at the fragmented world, turning
from the unbearable accusation in his eyes. Billy and
Gramps were now looking at her with stunned
betrayal writen in the lines of their disappointed
faces.

'My dear,' Clarice continued with a husky laugh,
'you look as if you didn't know Rae was working on
an article. For heaven's sake, it's about you!'

'About me?' Galen repeated flatly, his eyes
narrowing to dangerous slits. 'I can't think of a
single thing about me that would be of interest to a
woman's publication.'

'I assure you, Galen, that there are dozens of

things about you that would interest women——'
the words were spoken with a possessive and
blatantly sexual innuendo, 'but I was just a tiny bit
shocked to learn you'd placed an ad for a wife. I
suspected immediately, of course, that perhaps other
little minds had been busy behind the scenes.' She
treated Gramps and Billy to a scolding finger and a
patronising smile that forgave them their childish
high jinks, then deliberately widened her eyes on
Galen. 'But surely you knew why Miss Douglas was
here?' A slender hand covered a mouth that had
dropped delicately open in a fairly good imitation of
astonishment. 'Oh, dear,' she said softly, fluttering
her lashes in a fairly good imitation of distress.
'Have I committed a dreadful gaffe?'

Galen's eyes remained coldly and inscrutably on
Rae's face, though he addressed his next comment
to Clarice. 'So Ms Douglas is here researching an
article on the type of men who place ads looking for
wives?'

'Well, that was my understanding,' Clarice said
with a fairly good imitation of reluctance.

Galen's features tightened into a cold mask. His
eyes cooled to glacial. Only a leaping muscle in his
jaw gave away his tightly reined fury.

Outraged censure was growing in Billy's and
Gramps' gazes now as well.

'Oh, no,' Rae gasped weakly. 'That isn't it. That
isn't it at all. I mean, it was at first. But not now.
Not since I first realised you hadn't——' Her voice
trailed away dispiritedly. She tried desperately to
collect her thoughts. But Galen was not the tender
man who had held her so close and reverently last
night. The icily dangerous man who sat staring at
her unwinkingly was a complete stranger.

'Since you found out that Galen wasn't looking
for a wife,' Clarice finished her sentence for her. 'Of
course he's not. Why, we've been talking about
marriage for quite some time now, haven't we,
dear?'

The cry 'I was going to tell you' died in Rae's
throat, and her frantic need to defend herself
evaporated. It was her turn to look accusingly down
the length of the table. Suddenly she was the
betrayed, and not the betrayer. Withholding the fact
that she worked for a magazine was nothing in
comparison to what he had done! He had asked her
to marry him—when he was already practically
engaged to another woman! How could he? Was it
all just a game? Did he ask every woman who lay
down in the hay beside him to be his wife?

She felt an old and familiar bitterness come home
to roost. She had been fool enough to trust again, to
dream again, to believe again. She had made the
identical mistake she'd made before. She had
become so caught up in her romantic ideals that she
had not properly investigated her suspicions about
him and Clarice. She closed her eyes against the
almost nauseating pain that had begun at the pit of
her stomach and was creeping up towards her heart.

'I think I've heard enough, Clarice.' Galen's tone
was low and stern and weary. Rae felt a weak flutter
of hope within her breast. Could he really be coming
to her defence? Could he be believing what his heart
was telling him, rather than the evidence stacked up
against her? But no, the look on his face suggested
he was only protecting himself from being dragged
any further over the coals of deceit and betrayal. She
reminded herself bitterly that he was not the only
one who had been wronged.

With a sudden loud wail, Billy burst into tears, scrambled from his chair and faced Clarice furiously.

'You witch! I hate you! I hate you!' He turned and darted from the room, his sobs lingering pathetically in the charged silence left in his wake.

Rae wished she could childishly echo both his words and his exit, but instead she sat miserably looking at her fingers.

'Goodness, what's gotten into that child?' Clarice asked with affront, sending Rae a glance that found her guilty of influencing him in the worst possible way. 'I really think he should be made to apologise, Galen.'

Galen rose from the table. 'I think not,' he said coldly. 'I trust you can find your own way back, Clarice?'

'Galen, I——' Her voice faltered when a light flickered in Galen's coal-black eyes that could only be described as killing.

For the first time the woman's composed façade fell away. 'Well, I suppose,' she said uncertainly. Galen nodded curtly, his face frighteningly remote, and left the room.

Gramps glared at Clarice. 'Well, you finally seem to have cut your own pretty throat, but did you have to take a good woman down with you?'

'Oh, butt out, you old fool!' Clarice spat out, and then with obvious effort she stopped herself and smiled with cold composure at Gramps. 'He'll come around.'

'That I wouldn't count on,' Gramps growled.

Rae sent him a plaintive look. Did that go for both of them?

Gramps caught her look of abject misery and gave

her a faint smile. 'Count on it,' he said softly, and then he, too, left the room. There was a sag to his shoulders that made him look old and sad.

'I can't abide that meddlesome old man,' Clarice commented with veiled fury, and then turned a plastic smile on Rae. 'Well, Rae, by chance I have a helicopter landing some supplies today. I think, from the look Galen just gave you, you'll probably want to be on it.'

She nodded dully. What choice did she have? She couldn't bear the thought of facing Galen, of seeing him look at her again with indifferent contempt in the eyes that, just an hour ago, had warmed her with their tenderness.

'How did you find out about the article? And about the other?' Rae asked raggedly.

Clarice gave a low laugh. 'It was ridiculously easy. I called the magazine, posing as an old friend. That's when I was cheerfully informed you didn't work in the advertising department. I said I desperately wanted to see you before I left Calgary, and was put through to Sal. I played a hunch, then. I saw something in you when I first met you. A look that usually means a man. A bad man. So I asked Sal if you were still with your fellow. She was quite eager to give me the scoop on dear Roger, and how he had thankfully passed from your life, nearly ruining your career in the process. I must congratulate myself on ''oh''ing and ''ah''ing in all the correct places, because she was quite quick to confide in your dear friend about the assignment that was getting you back on track as a writer and as a woman.'

'Why?' Rae asked with bitter astonishment. 'Why would you go to the trouble of deceiving my boss? Why did you want to ruin me? You don't even know me.'

'As you know, I happened to see you and Galen in the bushes that day. Galen paid me a visit that night. He said he wouldn't be coming around for a while. That made me feel slightly threatened. And I don't like to feel threatened. Ever.'

Wouldn't be coming around for a while? What a skunk! Rae thought viciously. He had planned to play with her—but to leave his other hands open, too. Until when? Was he going to marry her, and then reopen his affair with Clarice? Couldn't one woman ever be enough for a man? She hated them all equally in that moment. She tried to feel only lucky that she had escaped in time. And yet she didn't. There was a small niggling doubt still. After all, Clarice had branded herself a liar out of her own mouth.

'And do you love Galen that much? That you would go to these lengths to have him? That you would destroy another human being in order to possess him?' But somehow she already knew—love did not destroy in its name, and no one would ever 'possess' the strong, proud, independent man that she loved. Yes, that she loved, even though she wanted desperately not to love him any more.

Clarice's eyes glinted with amusement. 'Love? You are a real babe in the woods, aren't you? No wonder old Roger Dodger had such a devastating effect on you. Love's for children—the silly stuff of fairy-tales. Don't get me wrong. I respect Galen immensely. He's one of the few men who isn't in the least intimidated by me. He's an attractive, intelligent, strong, sensual, stimulating man. That's a combination I've been searching for for a long

time. I'm not about to surrender five years of
groundwork to a wide-eyed wonder straight out of
Mary Poppins.'

'He deserves better than you,' Rae commented
absently, then wondered why she felt that way.
What he deserved was to be tarred and feathered!
He had proved he was no better than Roger. And
yet, despite the evidence, she knew at some deep
level she would never be able to totally convince
herself of that.

'Darling, there is no better than me,' Clarice
started in a husky, brazen tone. 'Now, go get your
things. Your little stay on Fantasy Island is over.'

CHAPTER ELEVEN

'OH, RAE!' Sal moaned plaintively. 'I want to jump right out the window! I can't believe the role I played in all this! If only you could have heard her! You probably would have believed yourself that she was your most bosom buddy! I can still hear her: "And that horrible boyfriend—what was his name?—is he still in the picture?" ' Sal sighed. 'And I can just hear myself—"He was married! And he nearly killed her, not to mention her career . . ." And then I just couldn't stop myself from telling her why she couldn't get in touch with you, and what I thought might be happening at the farm.' Sal moaned again, her eyes full of concern on Rae's wan features. 'How are you ever going to forgive me?'

'Sal, there's really not much to forgive you for,' Rae assured her quietly. 'Two people in very isolated and intense circumstances thought they fell in love. I guess if it couldn't withstand the first little test the outside world put it to, it probably wasn't ever what we thought it was anyway.'

'If Clarice Harmond's intervention can be called a "little" test, so can the dropping of the bomb at Bikini.' An indignant pout appeared on Sal's pretty features. 'Do you suppose he really asked her to marry him?'

'He didn't deny it,' Rae said wearily. But it was a question she had asked herself inside her head at least a million times. Unfortunately, no matter how

hard she tried to condemn Galen as being the same
as Roger, and all men for that matter, she could not
shake her original gut feeling that Galen was not
capable of compromising his integrity. The feeling
was self-defeating in that it kept a flicker of hope
alive inside her, kept her nerves strung tight as she
listened for the phone to ring, or for the sound of a
familiar tread outside her apartment door.

Last night, for the third night in a row, she had
stayed awake in her bed listening to every car that
stopped on the street three floors below, imagined it
might have been a truck, and then followed him in
her imagination as he moved from the truck to the
door, up in the lift, down the hall—and then she had
died a thousand deaths when the expected knock on
her door had not materialised. Died a thousand
deaths—and then, with the slamming of another car
door, started the whole self-defeating process over
again.

'Look, why don't you take a week off, putter
around with the article, relax a bit . . .'

'The article's done.' Rae felt a nervous qualm as
she handed the neatly typed manuscript to Sal. She
wished, not for the first time, that it had been ready
when she'd left the farm. She could have left a copy,
and maybe he would have seen her innocence in
every line. But her departure had been so
unexpected, and there had been simply no point in
leaving pages of very rough notes and snatches of
sunshine phrases and rainbow words that formed a
puzzle only she could put together. She had begun
work as soon as she had stumbled in from the farm.

It had taken her sixteen hours of non-stop work.
The pages represented a labour of complete
devotion. Once the notes were sorted out, every-

thing had begun to flow from her in a joyous outpour. It was as if, for a few hours more, she had found a way to cling to all she had come to love so deeply and desperately. Even in her state of near collapse when the rough was done, she knew she had done what she'd set out to do. She had captured something, and there was a potent magic in these neat white and black pages. But she had not stopped there.

Never had she gone over a piece of her writing so critically, stripping it mercilessly to its heart and soul, and then making sure that there was not even a flimsy piece of evidence that could link this article to the MacNamaras and violate their privacy.

And yet still she handed the sheaves of paper to Sal uncertainly. She was so close to this topic—perhaps too close. Maybe this story would just come across as the heartsick and ridiculous ramblings of a woman suffering the intense pain of having loved and lost. Maybe it would seem trivial and altogether too purple and poetic for a magazine with the tough professional standards of *Womanworld*. Maybe it wouldn't make any sense at all to the cosmopolitan readership . . .

Rae realised that, through this article more than any other she had ever written, she was holding up her heart and soul, the very essence of her being, to the scrutiny of other people. She had held back nothing, so if this effort was rejected, she had nothing left. And she had been totally rejected once already this past week. She wasn't strong enough to handle it again.

'Sal,' she suggested nervously, 'you don't have to read it now. Why don't you take it to your office and get back to me?' In a week, or a month, or a year, she added uneasily to herself.

An imperious hand was lifted for silence, and, rather than torture herself by watching Sal's changing expressions, Rae turned to the window.

Only a few short weeks had passed since she'd last looked out over this view, and yet the whole world had changed. Where there had only been grey before, now there were blue skies and patches of delicate newborn greens. Even the people in the street far below were dressed brightly, clothed in shouting rainbow colours that mirrored their spirited celebration of winter's end.

Rae sighed. She wondered if she would ever be able to appreciate the man-made and manicured beauty at the heart of a city again. She knew a different kind of beauty now—one that used space and silence as its canvas. How she yearned for that country landscape as she looked out over the bustling city. Yearned for the sight of fields broken by fences, and dotted with cattle, for the sight of red barns and log houses, for the sight of a giant of a man striding towards her, the wind ruffling bronze hair, a tender smile playing across chiselled, wind-burned features.

The canvas of her mind was filled in rapidly. Ah, yes, there was a boy, galloping a white horse across wide-open fields, and an old man gently watering the seedlings he grew with such care in the kitchen window.

Oh, God, Rae thought desperately, swiping frantically at her brimming eyes. She couldn't cry now. She couldn't. And yet the emptiness was welling up within her, a loneliness that felt like nothing she had ever felt. She wanted to go *home*. She wanted to return to the land she loved, to the people she loved, and especially to the man she loved. It couldn't have all been a fantasy. It couldn't be true that after being tantalised for the past few weeks with a vision of all the joy life could hold, she now had to settle for this—days full of nothingness, no matter what they held. A world without colour, no matter how cheerfully spring painted it. A heart without hope . . .

It's only been four days, she told herself, and then, to regain control, she comforted herself with the possibility that he would phone. He had to sooner or later. He had felt it, too. He couldn't just walk away from the golden promise they had glimpsed of what a life shared together would be like. He was strong, but not that strong. They had felt so many things with the same intensity. They had from the very beginning. So he would be feeling this too, with the same tragic sense of loss she was experiencing. He would be feeling the emptiness, the hollowness, the deathlike sense of grief. He *would* call. Wouldn't he?

'Rae.'

She struggled back to the surface of reality, braced herself, and turned to Sal.

There was a long silence and Sal looked at her appraisingly. 'It's the best you've ever done,' she said softly and sincerely. 'It's beautiful—it has a brilliant and hauntingly beautiful style—a richness and a depth you weren't capable of a year ago. Maybe not even a month ago. But it's the kind of writing I always hoped you would do some day.'

'Thank you,' Rae breathed, closing her eyes with relief.

'At the risk of sounding like an Old Mother Hubbard, let me tell you something, Rae. At the moment, you look as haggard as the mother of forty

ten-year-old boy scouts. And yet there's a glow in
your eyes I've never seen before. Real love
enriches—it doesn't carelessly mutilate hearts and
minds like so much paper going through the
shredder. And even though letting go of love is the
most painful of life's experiences, it still isn't
destructive. You'll find this hard to believe now, but
eventually this lesson of life will make you stronger,
gentler, more loving—better. Not bitter, and
disenchanted. I hope you can believe me.'

Rae's mind brushed tenderly over her memories.
And she knew in her heart that Sal spoke a basic
truth. In the end, having known Galen could only
enrich her as a human being—not tear her down.
She had had, for a few moments in time, what many
people would search for and never find in all their
lives. It was worth the price. The old adage was true.
It *was* better to have loved and to have lost than
never to have loved at all.

Besides, there was still the deep certainty in her
heart that Galen was going through all that she was
going through. And in the end he would call, and
give her a chance to explain Clarice's ugly
revelations. Just as she would give him a chance to
explain his relationship with Clarice. If there had
ever been something there, she felt confident there
no longer could be. Not now. Not after all they had
shared. And perhaps that was the bottom line—Rae
could not bring herself to believe she had been
betrayed by Galen, and this gave her hope.

Rae's certainty faded somewhat as a week stretched
into a month and Galen didn't make any effort to get
in touch with her. A thousand times or more she
reached for the telephone herself. Occasionally she

even started to dial the number she now knew by heart. But always her courage faded before she had finished dialling. She would recall the look of cold censure on his face when he had found out about her job and about Roger, and she would feel it was up to him to make the move.

Love had to involve trust. Love had to involve believing the best of your beloved. She wasn't certain that their relationship would be worth having if she had to talk him into believing the best of her, like some suave lawyer trying to win over a suspicious jury. A basic trust in his own feelings and in her had to be something he felt in his heart already, and an explanation would have to just act as a confirmation of those gut level feelings—not as the be all and end all.

He had to trust her the way she trusted him—after her initial sense of betrayal when Clarice had announced the supposed status of her relationship with Galen, she had simply known with her whole heart and soul that it was not true. Now, she expected at least that much from Galen.

Meanwhile she dragged through the days feeling oddly suspended in time. Waiting. Waiting. Waiting. Not quite alive, as if some essential part of her had been severed from her being. She had a strange sensation of being not quite complete. Her relationship with Galen had filled a place within her that she had not realised was empty. And yet now that place was an integral part of her. The emptiness where there had been such fullness filled her with a yearning that was excruciatingly painful—more painful than anything she had ever felt.

And yet, despite the emotional turmoil, the pain and the uncertainty she was going through, her writing was not suffering. In fact it had a quality and a depth that it had never had before—her spirit rising above pain, and slipping through her pen. In Sal's words, 'a brilliant and hauntingly beautiful style' had emerged as the result of the lessons of love.

When her piece, entitled simply 'A Country Day' appeared in *Womanworld*, Rae was overwhelmed and touched by the enthusiastic and emotional mail she received from their cosmopolitan readership. It was as if a small bouquet of flowers had risen from the ashes of her agony, and in this she found consolation. If she could touch others so deeply, perhaps her heartbreak was not totally without reason . . .

Rae looked up from an article she was rewriting and frowned. The receptionist, Mrs O'Cleary, stood inside her door looking breathless and flushed—quite a change from her general old-ironsides countenance.

'What is it, Mrs O'Cleary?' Rae asked, baffled when the woman made no move to say what she wanted.

'There's a gentleman here to see you, miss.' A girlish giggle escaped those usually tight-pursed lips. 'Well, a gentleman is probably stretching it a bit. An Irish rogue, the likes of which I haven't seen in years—could have spotted him a mile off, even though he is missing the old-country lilt in his voice. He's got that look in his eyes of pure devilment, and I tell you he's got the gift of the charm——'

Rae had stopped listening. Wordlessly, with the blood draining from her face, and with hope pounding hard at her heart, she got up and moved by the openly curious Mrs O'Cleary.

The hallway to the outer office seemed like the longest walk of her life. She forced her leaden legs to walk, because for all that they felt like dead weight, it would have been so easy to break into a run.

Part of her cautioned her against foolishly getting her hopes up. 'Whoa, Rae,' she told herself softly. 'The world is full of charming Irishmen.' But another part refused to listen to the stern voice of reason and was singing and doing cartwheels inside her.

He was leaning nonchalantly against Mrs O'Cleary's desk when Rae quietly entered the outer office. He was inspecting a painting on the wall beside him with apparent interest, though his fingers drummed an impatient tattoo on the desk-top. For a moment she could only stand, silently and helplessly, drinking in his clean, long lines with greedy need. Those lean and muscular legs had carried him along beside her, those sinewy arms had held her, those dark, mysterious eyes had feasted on her, those firm lips had branded her for all time.

'Galen,' she whispered, frozen in the doorway.

He swivelled towards her, his eyes as hungry on her as hers had been on him. Her first reaction on seeing his face full-on was shock. From Mrs O'Cleary's description she had not expected this—the weary lines around his eyes, the haggard pallor, the deep, troubled creases at the sides of his mouth. But then, she had always been able to see in Galen what others missed.

Tremulously she covered the distance between them and instinctively reached up with tender fingers that sought to erase the evidence of pain etched in his face.

He caught her hand before it touched his face, and the tears welled in her eyes. Her reaction was panicked—he was rejecting her! Why had he come all this way to reject her? His eyes, dark and impassive, seared her to her soul with their intensity and leashed passion. And then slowly, ever so slowly, he took her hand and placed it gently, reverently, to his lips.

Mrs O'Cleary giggled behind them, and Galen dropped her hand from his lips but not from his grasp.

He turned and gave the intruder a smile that was indeed devilish and charming and wondrous to behold. It erased the pain etched deep into his features and gave him the look of a bold adventurer who owned the very earth. It was the smile of a man victorious at love.

'Would you kindly tell Rae's boss she's been kidnapped?' His eyes found hers again. 'And if what I see in her eyes is what I think it is, it's quite possible she'll never return.'

'Tell Sal I'll freelance for her,' Rae managed to call over her shoulder as she was being pulled willingly from the office. Yes, freelancing would be an ideal career for a wife and a mother.

'Are you really kidnapping me?' she asked uncaringly as they took the lift down, and she snuggled comfortably under the familiar and welcome weight of his arm around her shoulder.

'Actually, this is a preliminary to the kidnapping. I thought I'd take you for a nice quiet lunch and we can try to work things out between us. If not,' he shrugged those incredible shoulders, and she noted blissfully he was every bit as enticing in his well-cut sports jacket as he had been in the ugly green workshirt that he favoured, 'if not, I will probably have to resort to kidnapping.'

'Let's get straight to the kidnapping,' she murmured happily. 'You might as well save your money. I wouldn't taste a thing I put in my mouth right now.'

'I wouldn't either,' he admitted, with an endearing grin. 'How about a ride in the get-away vehicle?' He guided her towards a beat-up truck that she recognised fondly, opened the door and helped her up.

'You're parked illegally,' she noted inanely.

'I know. But I'd driven around this block fifty times looking for a parking spot, and finally it was too much for me—being so close to seeing you again, and something like a stupid parking spot getting in the way. I finally just deserted the truck.'

'A good beginning to your career as an outlaw,' she commented lightly.

Galen pulled her across the seat towards him, placed a finger on her chin and lifted her eyes to his. 'Rae, oh, beautiful Rae. Can you ever forgive me? I can see in your eyes that I've hurt you, and nothing has ever made me sorrier.'

'I can see in your eyes that I wasn't the only one hurt,' she responded softly. 'Why did you wait so God-awful long, Galen? Why have you come now?'

'I waited so long because I'm a stubborn fool,' he said with a contrite smile. 'I waited so long because I thought history was repeating itself in the most painful way—that I had once again chosen a woman who was an accomplished actress, and a liar and a cheat. How anybody could look into your eyes and believe any of those things is beyond me. But maybe because I didn't have your eyes there to look into,

I was convincing myself more each day that you weren't ever what you had appeared to be. I told myself that if you weren't a complete fraud, if you hadn't just used me, you would call—or come back. That you would defend yourself against the charges.'

'I couldn't, Galen,' she explained quietly, 'I couldn't come back on those terms—hoping the strength of an argument could win you. I had to know that your own heart won you.' She looked at him uncertainly, her joy feeling suddenly precarious. 'Galen, you are here because you want to be, aren't you? You aren't buckling under from pressure from Billy and Gramps?'

Galen smiled. 'Believe me, there's been enough of that to buckle a plough-horse. But no, they aren't why I'm here.'

'Then what convinced you to come? After all this time?'

He reached across her and opened the glove box. He pulled out a copy of *Womanworld*. 'You did.'

She looked uncomprehendingly at the magazine.

'It was so clear. In between every single line of "A Country Day" I read the truth. Not just that you loved the farm, but that you loved me. The whole article is so pure, it shines. Nobody could pretend feelings like that. And nobody could ever feel the agony that I felt when I read it and came face to face with what a fool I had been.'

'But what if you had never read it?' she forced herself to ask.

'But that's impossible,' he told her softly. 'Destiny had its hand in this from the beginning. It wouldn't be thwarted.'

She studied the magazine uncomfortably. 'There

are things I should have told you about sooner,' she admitted quietly. 'About the article—about Roger.'

'No, Rae. Those are just surface things. Details. What you are, your soul, doesn't need words or explanations. I can see it in your eyes. If you want to tell me some day, that's fine. But the telling will be for you, not for me, is that clear?'

She nodded, elation building within her. 'I feel that way too—about your involvement with Clarice.'

He snorted. 'There is no involvement with Clarice. I won't say there never was, though what there was now seems a small and meaningless thing. At one point she did instigate some discussion on marriage. I'll admit I even considered it, but thank God, I found out how much more there could be before I ever committed myself.

'She's gone, Rae. She sold her place last week, after finally realising I meant what I said to her that night at her place. That I'd fallen in love. And that I'd never be back. That didn't change when you left. For betrayed as I felt by you, I couldn't forgive her for the hurt she'd inflicted on us.'

'Galen,' Rae said softly. 'I need very badly to be kissed.'

'Hmm. Funny thing—so do I.' He folded her into his arms, and their lips met. A busy downtown street faded into oblivion, and they were unaware and uncaring of the amused looks of passers-by.

They might have stayed that way for a good long time, except for the sudden rapping on the window.

They both turned to see an annoyed policeman.

'Come on, buddy. You can't park here.'

Galen gave him a salute, gave Rae another kiss, and started the truck.

'Where are we going?'

'We're going to get a marriage licence, and then we're going to get married, and then we're going on a honeymoon.'

'Galen?'

'What?'

'Could we skip the honeymoon, and just go home?'

He looked at her with delighted surprise. 'Is that really what you want?'

'More than the earth,' she said with a firm nod.

'That's how much I love you,' he mused. 'More than the earth.' He started to kiss her again, but pulled away abruptly when the cars behind him started to honk. 'I can't wait to get you on a quiet country lane,' he complained. 'Meanwhile, I guess it would be OK if you opened your wedding present from Billy.'

She found the painstakingly wrapped gift tucked under the seat. Underneath an excess of tissue paper was an elaborately decorated cook book that had obviously been made at school. Each child had written out and illustrated his favourite recipe.

'The Mother's Day gift,' she guessed, 'that started the wheels in motion for this whole experience.' She flipped through it, looking for Billy's contribution.

Her eyes misted with tears. On the final page was her own recipe for chocolate chip cookies, printed in Billy's hand.

'By Billy's new mom, Rae,' the caption read confidently.

'He never doubted for a moment,' Galen said softly. 'Even when Mother's Day came and went. He never showed it to me. He hid it in his room.

Poor kid. I think he probably took it out and prayed
over it every night.'

'To answered prayers,' she whispered, touching
her lips to the cover of the book.

Without her realising it, Galen had left the city
and now they drew to a halt on a country lane,
shaded with delicate new green leaves. She went into
his waiting arms and met his waiting lips, and
somehow in that kiss she knew that spring had come
for all time.

ROMANCE

Next month's romances from Mills & Boon

Each month, you can choose from a world of variety in romance with Mills & Boon. These are the new titles to look out for next month.

Mills & Boon
the rose of romance

AND THEN HE KISSED HER...

This is the title of our new venture — an audio tape designed to help you become a successful Mills & Boon author!

In the past, those of you who asked us for advice on how to write for Mills & Boon have been supplied with brief printed guidelines. Our new tape expands on these and, by carefully chosen examples, shows you how to make your story come alive. And we think you'll enjoy listening to it.

You can still get the printed guidelines by writing to our Editorial Department. But, if you would like to have the tape, please send a cheque or postal order for £4.95 (which includes VAT and postage) to:

VAT REG. No. 232 4334 96

- -

AND THEN HE KISSED HER...
To: Mills & Boon Reader Service, FREEPOST, P.O. Box 236, Croydon, Surrey CR9 9EL.

Please send me _____ copies of the audio tape. I enclose a cheque/postal order*, crossed and made payable to Mills & Boon Reader Service, for the sum of £ _____ . *Please delete whichever is not applicable.

Signature _____

Name (BLOCK LETTERS) _____

Address _____

_____ Post Code _____

AROUND THE WORLD WORDSEARCH
COMPETITION!

How would you like a years supply of Mills & Boon Romances ABSOLUTELY FREE? Well, you can win them! All you have to do is complete the word puzzle below and send it in to us by October 31st. 1989. The first 5 correct entries picked out of the bag after that date will win **a years supply of Mills & Boon Romances** (*ten books every month - **worth around £150**) What could be easier?

R	D	N	A	L	R	E	Z	T	I	W	S
E	O	N	M	C	H	I	N	A	A	C	C
G	M	U	I	G	L	E	B	N	N	U	O
Y	E	C	E	G	W	H	I	Z	C	B	T
P	D	R	H	S	E	R	I	A	Z	A	L
T	N	S	M	P	E	R	U	N	D	D	A
N	A	W	I	A	T	P	I	I	E	N	N
Y	L	A	T	I	N	A	N	A	N	A	D
N	G	S	T	N	H	Y	D	E	M	L	Q
W	N	O	J	A	M	A	I	C	A	L	A
R	E	L	A	D	A	N	A	C	R	O	R
T	H	A	I	L	A	N	D	D	K	H	I

ITALY	THAILAND	SCOTLAND	SWITZERLAND
GERMANY	IRAQ	JAMAICA	
HOLLAND	ZAIRE	TANZANIA	**PLEASE TURN**
BELGIUM	TAIWAN	PERU	**OVER FOR**
EGYPT	CANADA	SPAIN	**DETAILS**
CHINA	INDIA	DENMARK	**ON HOW**
NIGERIA	ENGLAND	CUBA	**TO ENTER**

HOW TO ENTER

All the words listed overleaf, below the word puzzle, are hidden in the grid. You can find them by reading the letters forward, backwards, up or down, or diagonally. When you find a word, circle it or put a line through it, the remaining letters (which you can read from left to right, from the top of the puzzle through to the bottom) will spell a secret message.

After you have filled in all the words, don't forget to fill in your name and address in the space provided and pop this page in an envelope (you don't need a stamp) and post it today. Hurry - competition ends October 31st. 1989.

Mills & Boon Competition,
FREEPOST,
P.O. Box 236,
Croydon,
Surrey. CR9 9EL
Only one entry per household

Secret Message _____

_____

Name _____

Address _____

_____

_____

_____ Postcode _____

You may be mailed as a result of entering this competition

mps
*MAILING
PREFERENCE
SERVICE*

COMP 6